Born To Be Devilish

(Book 2 of the Demon Employment series)

Born To Be Wicked – Book 1
Born To Be Devilish – Book 2
Born To Be Badass – Book 3

Shade Owens
www.shadeowens.com

Edited by Nikki Busch
www.nikkibuschediting.com

RED RAVEN PUBLISHING

Chapter 1

Staring up at the ceiling's intricate swirls, I can't help but wonder: how long will this last? It feels like I'm living a fantasy, which is saying a lot coming from a thousand-year-old succubus.

This isn't the first time I've stayed in Las Vegas's Bellagio hotel, but being here next to Veerka makes me feel like I've been reborn. Maybe staying in the most expensive presidential suite has something to do with that, too.

She presses her icy skin against my body, her bright blue—almost white—eyes fixated on me. Slowly, her white hand creeps out from underneath our silk sheet, and she glides one of her sharp fingernails along my collarbone. I wince as her nail scratches off some of my skin, but I don't want her to stop. If anything, I want her to press harder. It makes me feel alive.

When she reaches my bare chest, goose bumps explode all over my body. "What're you thinking about, darling?"

You, I want to say.

"Lucius," I admit.

The last person I want to be thinking about while lying naked next to my long-lost lover who, for the last two centuries I thought was dead, is her current boyfriend. Lucius Retnich—the vampire leader of San Halos. He also happens to be pretty damn close to Asmodeus, the oldest and most respected vampire of all time.

Well, I'm not so sure he's still the most *respected*, but he is the most feared. Some vampires even view him as a god. He's been around since the beginning, and he's the one who makes all the rules and laws for the vampires of the world.

When my boss, Jamieson, gave me my latest job, he offered me five million big ones for Veerka's head. I had no idea Veerka was the woman I once knew as Elizabeth over two hundred years ago. Her being a vampire was a bit of a surprise, too, but it hasn't taken me long to accept it.

I'm happy living as a succubus. Way back when, I didn't have full control over my power, so having sex with Veerka wasn't even a possibility.

Now, we have a lot of catching up to do.

"What about him?" Veerka asks. This time, she runs her fingers through my long black hair and plays with its ends.

It's been about a week since Veerka and I took off from the Lotus Hotel—the spot where I was supposed to kill her. Instead, we faked her death and I cut ties with Jamieson after he transferred me three million dollars. He owed me five, but whatever.

The prick can keep the rest.

He wanted Veerka's sapphire necklace, something he called the Eye of Poseidon. I haven't questioned her on it yet, but I will.

It's what happened after I got my money that keeps replaying in my mind... The way Veerka climbed backward onto the California king bed, her naked body looking like snow against the royal purple sheets. And then the way she lay there, watching my hungrily...

"He must be looking for you," I say, my mouth drying up at the memory.

"Of course he is," she says. "But what does that matter?"

With all her fingers this time, she scratches downward on my chest, leaving five pink lines, and squeezes my left breast.

I want to talk about the fact that we haven't even discussed our plan to take down Asmodeus, but I can't think straight. I'm the succubus—I'm the one who's supposed to suck all the life out of people, not the other way around. Her chilly hand slips under the silk sheet and she slides downward over my belly, along my hip, and in between my legs. When her fingernails reach my inner thigh, my eyes close and it feels like the entire room is spinning.

Then, one torturous touch at a time, she walks

her fingers back up between my legs.

Right before she reaches where I want her to, a loud gunshot explodes down the hall. My eyes pop open and I turn to Veerka.

"Did you hear that?" I hiss.

She rolls her eyes as if I asked her to get up and make me a sandwich. Pulling away, she rolls off the bed. "Guess that's our cue."

I lie there for a few seconds, waiting for my brain to turn back on and imagining what I'll do to the shooter when I see them.

Fucking bastard.

I was so close.

So goddamn close.

Another gunshot goes off, and this time, it's followed by a crowd of people screaming.

Veerka slips into the same dress she wore last night—a lace, knee-length dress that makes her eyes pop even more. I have enough time to grab my leather jacket when the hotel room's door bursts open and in come two huge vampires with thick faces, black suits that look too tight for their bodies, and bloody chins. They look so much alike I can only assume they're twins.

But what the hell are they doing? Everyone knows that vampires aren't supposed to make themselves known to feebles, and here they are with blood on their faces. But what did they do? Attack feebles out in the open for everyone to see? And the Bellagio hotel isn't a shadow dweller hotel—that's reserved for the Dark Hall, a hotel designed for all shadow dwellers to walk about freely.

I sigh. Maybe Veerka's right. Things will only get worse from here on out as vampires try to take over.

The vampire on the right opens his mouth wide, revealing long bloody fangs underneath deep pink gums. He lets out a loud hissing sound and globs of blood and saliva sprinkle out into the air as the sound fills the room.

The next thing I know, my black wings are wide open on either side of me and my silver succubus hair hangs over my shoulders. Every time I get caught off guard or feel like I'm in danger, I automatically reveal my true self.

Hissing back, I extend my long, black-nailed fingers, prepared to tear off some faces, when I glimpse Veerka rushing toward the window. What's she doing? Everyone knows the Las Vegas windows don't open. Some people refer to Las Vegas as the Suicide Capital of America. I don't even have the time to tell her though. Using her fist, she punches the window and it breaks apart into a bunch of fragments. With her arms, she scrapes the sides to create a clean opening. The shards cut her skin, staining the window frame with black blood, but she doesn't seem to care at all.

At once, both vampires lunge forward, but I don't give them enough time to reach her. With my wings, I flap as hard as I can toward them, creating a powerful gust that knocks them down on their asses.

It doesn't hurt them, but it's enough to buy me a few seconds.

Veerka looks back at me, a devious smile on her face that says, *Exactly like old times.*

Without hesitating, I propel myself into the air and straight toward the open window. Wrapping my arm around Veerka's waist, I send us both flying out of the Bellagio hotel's thirty-fourth story.

CHAPTER 2

As we fall through the night sky and toward a multitude of colorful lights, massive jets of water come spitting out of the Fountains of Bellagio. I flap my wings in time to dodge the powerful spray of water, and Veerka laughs in my arms.

Is she insane? How is any of this funny? Vampires are after her, and here she is, laughing her head off.

With a few more powerful flaps, I fly us to the top of the Bellagio hotel, at the far end, where we no one can see us and land against the hard surface. Veerka stumbles out of my arms with a hand over her mouth and small slits for eyes.

"That... that was incredible," she says.

She's laughing so hard I can't help but smile. I forgot how much Veerka loves a good thrill.

"Those were Lucius's men, weren't they?" I ask.

She nods, but she's still laughing. Then, she waves a hand in the air as if trying to erase or dismiss the fact that Lucius wants her back. "Oh, live a little, Alexis."

"Why were they after you?" I ask. "How does Lucius even know you're still alive? We faked your death, remember?"

Finally, she stops laughing and clears her throat. Slowly, the smile on her face disappears like a mint fizzing away in a glass of pop.

Isn't Veerka also a leader? When Jamieson asked me to kill her, he told me Veerka and Lucius were a power couple—that the two of them were dangerous and that they were changing the Underworld.

"Lucius knows things, Alexis. He knows I'm not dead. He may not understand where I've gone or what happened, but he knows I'm very much alive. He's tracking me because he wants me back."

"Wants you *back*? Isn't it your choice? Not like the two of you are married," I say.

If this conversation had nothing to do with Veerka, I'd laugh at the thought of two vampires getting married.

She averts her gaze, which leads me to believe there's something she isn't telling me.

"You two aren't a power couple, are you?" I ask.

She turns away, crosses her arms as if she's cold—which, obviously, she isn't considering she's a vampire—and leans the weight of her body against the wall behind her. Even after a few centuries, I can still tell when Veerka's got something on her mind. It's almost like no time has passed between us at all.

"Talk to me," I say.

"I'm nothing but décor, Alexis," she says at last. "With everything that's going on these days, Lucius wanted a woman by his side to appeal to both sexes. Female vampires are getting sick of being bossed around by men, so I'm the pretty face that makes them think I'm representing them."

"Why *you*?" I ask.

It sounds harsh coming out of my mouth, and that's not at all what I intended. Veerka is jaw-droppingly gorgeous, but I'm wondering why out of thousands of vampires out there, Lucius is so adamant about having her by his side.

"He thinks he loves me," she says.

I'm about to make some comment about how it's impossible for vampires to love anyone, when I remember that Veerka's a vampire. So instead, I bite my lower lip. "*Thinks?*"

"He's controlling," she says. "He makes all the decisions and gets me to announce them."

She won't even make eye contact. This isn't the Veerka I found in the hotel room last week. When she talks about him, all her confidence is gone.

"Is that why Jamieson wanted you dead? He thought you were the one causing all the changes?"

She smiles at me, but it isn't a happy smile—it's a look that says, *Come on, Alexis, you're smarter than that.*

When I say nothing, her smile fades. "You honestly don't know, do you?"

I get a knot in my stomach. Goddamn it. I hate big dark secrets. This is why I do things when I want, how I want. I like to feel like I'm in control of something, and the only time I'm okay not being in control is when I'm drunk.

Do I even want to know the truth?

"Jamieson isn't who you think he is," she says.

"Well, no shit," I say, recalling how he spoke to me last time. That's why I told him to go fuck himself. He's a greedy asshole who will step on anyone's back to get what he wants. Now that I know that, I refuse to work for him.

"I'm not referring to his personality," she says.

I arch a brow.

"He's working with Lucius, Alexis."

Now I need a drink.

I'm too shocked to say anything, so I don't. Instead, I pace back and forth as a mighty breeze sends my hair flying all over the place.

"Alexis, sit down," Veerka says.

"No. This doesn't make any sense. Jamieson... Jamieson doesn't work with the Underworld. He doesn't like it. Wants nothing to do with it. This... This makes no sense. I mean, I know he's a prick. But this would change everything I thought I knew about—"

"Alexis, sit down." She folds her arms across her chest.

I stop pacing at the sound of her authoritative voice.

When I look back at her, she jabs a finger next to her and stares me cold in the face. Sighing, I make my way over, press my back against the wall, and slide my way down.

"How do you know?" I ask.

She turns to look at me but stays silent. It's a look that says, *Do I seriously need to explain everything?*

It's also enough for me to believe her. She's always beside Lucius, which means she's privy to information that no one else is.

"Lucius has refused to pursue certain changes because of me," she says.

"What do you mean?"

"We fight all the time, Alexis. He's constantly working alongside Jamieson and making changes behind Asmodeus's back. I've told him I don't agree with certain things, like allowing vampire parents to turn their children. I assume word's gotten back to Jamieson that I'm the one standing in the way of his changes."

"That's why he wants you dead," I say, matter-of-factly.

She remains quiet, which says it all for me. How did I not see it? How has Jamieson been playing me this whole time? I guess my whole *don't ask, don't tell* policy goes both ways.

"Jamieson's dangerous, Alexis."

While I already knew that, I didn't realize how dangerous he truly was. I mean, I knew it was bad, but I had no idea he was involved with vampires. That makes things way more complicated.

Does he know about me? Does he know I'm a succubus? If he does, he's hidden it pretty damn well these last few years.

"Let me worry about Jamieson," I say. "If he comes anywhere near you, I'll fucking kill him."

The corner of her lip twitches like it's on the verge of forming a smile.

"What're we doing, Veerka? Are you going back to Lucius?"

"I have to," she says, and I clench my fists. "The only way I'll get anything done is by having insider information."

I know she's right—she can't stay on the run. In time, Lucius will catch up to her, and it's better that he thinks she got kidnapped than know she ran away. She needs to keep playing her part.

"I need you to do me a favor," she says.

I stare at her.

"San Halos has a few underground vampire groups preparing to stand up against Lucius. He doesn't know about them, and if he does, he severely underestimates them."

"Groups opposed to the Vampire Code?" I ask.

She nods.

The Vampire Code is the law established by Asmodeus. While Lucius enforces it, he's been bending several rules with Jamieson's help and finding ways to justify them. I guess vampires, like feeble citizens, are sick of old, archaic ways. It's no wonder they're pissed off. Rules haven't changed for several centuries, while everyone else has.

"I want you to find Devania Arkis," she says. "You must be discreet in your search and look for the Black Widow. If anyone asks, tell them Phoenix sent you."

"Whoa, hold up," I say. "Who is this chick? And what's up with the code language?"

Veerka smirks. "Devania is the woman we need to help us fight this battle. Don't worry—she won't be *too* hard to find."

"I don't get it," I say bluntly. Veerka isn't one to talk gibberish, but right now, she isn't making a whole lot of sense to me. I get the feeling she's only giving me half of the information, and I'm not sure why.

For a split second, my stomach tightens, and I can't help but wonder if Veerka's playing both sides. Is this a setup? It doesn't feel like it, but when it comes to Veerka, I can't trust my gut. Unfortunately, seeing her again has messed me up. For the first time in as long as I can remember, I can feel my emotions.

I'll need more than a drink to get rid of this.

But at the same time, I don't want to get rid of it.

"You need to be more specific, Veerka. Who is this chick? And where do I even start looking?"

"If you want to find her, you will," Veerka says

plainly.

I cross my arms and raise both eyebrows—a look intended to say, *Finish answering my question.*

That sexy smirk creeps back onto her lips and I can't help but let my gaze fall to her breasts, her hips, and her thighs.

"Devania is the leader of the underground rebellion."

My eyes shoot back up and my jaw drops—literally. I wasn't born yesterday. Everyone knows several underground rebellion groups are working together to take down the vampires who run the show. They've been around for centuries, and no one knows how it started.

"Which group?" I blurt. "San Halos?"

Veerka shakes her head. "All of them."

My stare lingers. How does she even know this Devania woman? If she's working with Lucius, how could she be in contact with his enemy?

I can't hold it in. "How do you even know about these groups? You're supposed to be against them."

She tilts her head, her smile never fading. "I created them."

CHAPTER 3

There's so much running through my mind. I get why Veerka wants me to look for this Devania chick, but what I don't understand is why Veerka would continue to associate with someone who runs the underground rebellion. If Lucius finds out about this, she's a dead woman... and for good this time.

I'm also dying to know what happened to Veerka way back then. I saw it with my own eyes—the castle crumbled on her. How on Earth did Devania save her from that?

I have so many questions that I can't decide where to start, so instead, I mumble, "Devania Arkis."

Veerka pulls her long blond hair over one shoulder and nods. "We used to work together. I was her right hand, if you will. Well, before I left."

"Before you met Lucius," I say matter-of-factly.

She tugs at her hair again, which leads me to believe she still has ties to this woman.

"Precisely," she says. "But once I met Lucius, it

became clear to me..."

I watch her as she speaks, but I don't take any of it in. Instead, her words jumble together in one long, incoherent ramble and I can't help but smirk. "You sneaky little bitch."

She stops talking at once and pulls her face back as if I backhanded her and insulted her entire family.

"You infiltrated the Vampire Mafia," I say.

She doesn't smile, but there's a glimmer in her eye that confirms it all for me.

"How the hell did you keep this from Lucius? The man has people everywhere. Surely, someone out there knows who you are." As the words come out of my mouth, the gravity of the situation hits me. "Have you lost your mind, Veerka? How long can you keep this going? What's gonna happen when Lucius finds out? Not only will you have betrayed him... you'll have taken away his love." I slap my forehead. "Wow, you must have this vampire wrapped around your little pinky to be able to get away—"

Veerka points a stiff finger at me. "That's why he had better not find out. If you so much as breathe a word of this, Alexis, I'm dead."

I'm about to make a joke about her already *being dead*, but I can tell she's not in the mood. And now, I understand why. This is serious. She's a traitor to the most powerful people in all of San Halos. They've made an example of anyone who's ever crossed Lucius—some were torn apart by fishhooks, one tiny piece at a time, and others dipped into buckets of acid.

As horrible as that sounds, it's even worse for a vampire since they don't die. Instead, they're reduced to a skeleton held together by a few pieces of muscle and left to suffer until Lucius gets bored with them. After that, he severs their heads. Someone once told me he's even allowed some of his victims to recover, only to repeat the same torturous cycle again and again like a cat playing with a half-eaten mouse.

He's one sick son of a bitch, and if he finds out that the woman he loves has been deceiving him this whole time, well, I don't even want to imagine what he'll do to her.

"Relax," I say. "Your secret's safe with me."

She's anything but relaxed and neither am I. The rebellion is a massive group. It's comprised of multiple groups around the world, and there are bound to be a few traitors and rats. This also means that anyone in need of something from Lucius won't hesitate to use Veerka as blackmail.

Although I don't voice my concerns aloud, I feel them in the pit of my stomach. Veerka's fucked. Totally, entirely, and utterly fucked. If she tries to leave Lucius, he'll kill her, and if he finds out the truth, he'll kill her.

There's one way out of this that won't involve losing Veerka for good.

I cross my arms, which always makes me feel as tough as I am. "It's fine. We'll fix this, okay?"

She stares at me and bites her plush bottom lip. If she were still human and emotional, her eyes would probably start to water right about now.

I shrug as a way of making my next words come across as a piece of cake, when in reality I'm in way over my head. "We're going to take that fucker down."

This seems to soothe her, which is what I was going for. I can comb through the details later and figure out a master plan. She runs her hands through her hair, closes her eyes, and lets out a sharp breath. "Yeah, you're right. We have to tough this out a bit longer until Devania and the rebellion—"

Suddenly, a blinding blue light flashes in front of us and I shield my eyes with my forearm. Despite my attempt to protect my eyes, I have to blink dozens of times to regain my sight. At first, the apparition is hazy... almost like a cloud. But the shape morphs into a giant blue ball of electricity before swirling into a large oval the size of a car. As the colorful swirls spin around the center, Las Vegas begins to look like rainbow-colored paint being mixed in a can.

I recognize that shape, and those lights: it's magic.

Without warning, Drax comes bursting out of the portal, swinging his massive arms as if trying to swim through the air. If he weren't my best friend, I'd have thought him to be some dragon demon with that green scaly skin of his.

As he comes tumbling toward us, Veerka and I jump to our feet—me, out of confusion, and Veerka, in preparation for a fight. She parts her crimson lips, a catlike hiss aimed at Drax. The moment he sees her, he instinctively pulls his upper lip over his giant row of incisors—a look I rarely have the pleasure of seeing.

"Guys!" I shout, and Veerka and Drax turn toward me, the aggression on their faces vanishing as fast as it appeared.

Slowly, Veerka unclenches her fists, no doubt sensing that I know him.

But before she can interrogate me on who this lizard-man is, I throw my arms over my head. "What the hell are you doing here, Drax?"

He gasps hard to catch his breath and points backward into the portal. But before he can explain anything, a thick leather book comes hurling out of the portal and hits him square in the face. His big head rocks back and his eyes go crossed, then the stumbling starts up again.

The book lands hard on the floor, making a smacking sound.

Shit.

The *Book of Origin*.

The same book I may or may not have stolen from Rachel, the inexperienced teenage witch. I promised to give it back to her if she helped me reach Veerka with her portal. She did exactly that, so Drax gave her the book about a week ago. So what the fuck is going on? Why is he stumbling out of one of Rachel's portals with her book?

A high-pitched scream fills the air around us and out from the portal comes Rachel. I'd recognize that wiry, port-red hair anywhere, along with that little minion of hers, Riskus.

She waves a stick in the air—maybe it's a wand—and shouts something that sounds like a mixture of Latin and Russian. Maybe it's Witch Speak. Who knows? Beside her, Riskus does the same, only without a wand. He reaches into a leather pouch on his belt, extracts a purple powder, and throws the dust at the swirling portal.

Rachel jabs her wand into the gaping hole and shouts, "*Exitrus!*"

At once, the portal flickers, but right before it's about to close, a huge red talon comes reaching through it, its massive claw catching Rachel's shirt.

Holy mother of...

One of its claws alone is half the size of Rachel's body. She screams as the tip of it pulls her by the shirt, dragging her backward and into the closing portal.

"Master!" Riskus shouts.

He throws himself at her leg, but he's too small and light to be of any help at all. Instead, he gets dragged along with her, squealing and kicking his tiny childlike legs.

Drax and I bolt toward them. As I extract my wrist blades, Drax grabs Rachel around the torso, digs his feet claws into the roof's cement, and pulls back as hard as he can as if playing a game of tug-of-war. It doesn't do much, but it's enough to slow everything down.

With my blade, I slice downward through Rachel's shirt right before she disappears into the swirling hole. She falls flat on her butt, as do Riskus and Drax, and with a soft swoosh, the portal disappears, along with the monstrous talon.

Before any of them can go on about how *none of this was their fault*, I slap one hand on my right hip and glare down at all three of them. "What in the actual fuck?"

Veerka's eyes narrow on me. "For Christ's sake, Alexis, she's only a child."

"Only a child?" I say, mimicking her British accent. At once, I realize how petty and condescending this is, so I stop doing it. "She's a fuckin' witch is what she is!"

Veerka hisses, her lips curling over her upper teeth.

"Oh, right," I say. "I forgot how witches and vampires are taught to hate each other."

Rachel crosses her arms over her chest and stares back at Veerka like she's trying to challenge her. I don't get what her deal is. It's not like she knows anything about vampires, so she has no reason to hate them. But I suppose Veerka's aggressive stance is enough to put Rachel on guard.

"Would you two relax?" I say. "We're all on the same page. And speaking of pages, what the fuck, Rachel? What're you doing here, and why's your stupid book at my feet?"

"It isn't stupid," she says, her voice full of her typical teenage attitude. She reaches down, scoops up her book with both arms, and scowls at me.

My gaze shifts over to Drax, who raises his hands to either side of his face as if to say, *I didn't do anything.*

"Would someone please tell me what the hell's going on?" I snap.

Rachel points a finger at Drax. "It's his fault!"

Drax crosses his arms and scowls like a five-year-old.

"Drax?" I say, trying hard to keep calm.

He throws a hand toward Rachel. "One of the pages fell out of the book in your apartment. It must have come out when I pulled it out of your closet last week. So she"—he narrows his eyes with even more intensity at Rachel—"decides to come looking for it with no warning. I was in the middle of watching *Breaking Bad*, high out of my mind, when she appeared in front of the fucking television. Scared the shit out of me."

I turn to Rachel. "You portaled into my apartment uninvited?"

She shrugs. "It's an important page. I couldn't

find it anywhere in my room, so I figured maybe it fell out at your place."

Pinching the bridge of my nose, I sigh and turn back to Drax.

"Anyways, I found it," he continues. "The paper was blank and old-looking, so I don't get what she was freaking out about."

"It wasn't blank," Rachel says coldly. "It was a protection spell."

"No, it was bl—"

"Maybe to you, because you're a freaking lizard demon who can't read magic!"

"Guys!" I shout.

"Someone started knocking hard on your door," Drax continues. "I mean, it sounded like your landlord at first. You know how he gets. But then it got pretty bad and the door started shaking. So, Rachel here panicked and started reading off the sheet of paper in her hands. I thought she was making shit up, but I guess not." He wipes a line of sweat from his scaly forehead. "It all happened so fast. This pack of four vampire dudes broke down your door—"

"My door!" I snap.

"Alexis," Veerka says, and I realize I'm being a bit ridiculous given the fact that the three of them almost died.

"Yeah, they broke it down," Drax says. "They were vampires, Alex. Since when do vampires want anything to do with you?"

"Fucking Jamieson," I say under my breath.

"What?" Drax asks.

"Nothing, keep going."

"So, when they burst in, Rachel here finished reading her spell or whatever, and this huge fucking griffin with red feet and a red beak appeared in your apartment! It was so damn big, Alex. It could barely move around."

"I panicked," Rachel chimes in.

"You panicked?" I repeat.

"I created a portal with the bit of powder I had left from last time, and, well, it took us to you."

Stretching my neck sideways, I feel a soothing snap. "Great. This is fucking awesome."

Drax and Rachel exchange a look.

Why are they looking at each other like that? What the hell else is going on that I don't know about?

"Come on, spit it out!" I say.

"There's something else," Rachel says.

No shit.

I clench my jaw.

"When the griffin started freaking out inside your apartment, it snapped its beak at me and knocked my book out of my hands."

What is she talking about? She's holding the book against her chest, so what could be the problem?

Then, pulling it away from her chest, she opens it up. Inside, it looks like half the pages are missing.

"The tip of its beak sliced right through it and a bunch of papers went flying out before I grabbed it again."

Admittedly, I'm freaking out inside and about ready to fly down to the Las Vegas strip and get wasted. I can't deal with this shit.

"Are you telling me," I say through gritted teeth, "that the vampires who were looking for me now have half of the *Book of Origin* in their possession? A book which, let me remind you in case that thick skull of yours forgot, is the most powerful book known to shadow dwellers?"

With tight lips, she nods fast like a kid caught doing something wrong.

You have got to be fucking kidding me.

Chapter 4

"How long am I supposed to hang out in Las Vegas?" Rachel asks.

"As long as it takes," I say. "Now that those vampires have half the *Book of Origin*, someone will hunt you down for the rest of the book any time now."

Veerka crosses her arms and stares at Rachel. "She's a witch. Can't she place some sort of protective spell on the thing?"

Rachel glares at her. It's apparent that she's tired of people thinking she can do anything with her magic, and I don't blame her—the girl's still learning. Half the time, she guesses her spells. I'm willing to bet if she tries to put a protective spell on the book, it'll blow up in flames.

"Well, you can't keep walking around with that thing in your arms," Veerka adds. "Do you have any idea how dangerous—"

"I know," Rachel cuts her off. "Alexis told me. I get it, okay? This thing's powerful. It's not like it's my fault the damn griffin tore it to shreds."

"Well—" Drax says, his tone heightening in pitch.

Rachel glares at him.

"There's no use arguing about this," I say, losing my patience. "Rachel, Drax, and you—" I point to Riskus. "You guys come with me. We're going to see the Great Witch, Zerachu."

The corner of Rachel's lip pulls up. "Zerachu? Is that some sort of Pokémon?"

I make my eyelids go flat. What's her problem? Why does she always have to make stupid comments? It's like she enjoys the negative attention.

"You'd better show some respect if you want to meet one of the most powerful witches I know," I say.

This shuts her up.

I'm hesitant about bringing Rachel and the *Book of Origin* to Zerachu because I know what she'll say: "Vat da fuck is wrong with you, Alexis?"

Letting Rachel keep her damn book was beyond stupid. All right, taking it in the first place was the stupid part. But I was torn between not wanting the kid to kill herself and not wanting anything to do with the book. Zerachu won't miss a beat with me—she'll make sure I understand *exactly* how stupid I was. She'll say something like, "You foolish twit! Vy did you not bring the book to me?"

The funny thing about Zerachu is that she sounds like a vampire, but she looks like an old hag.

I guess that's stereotyping—not all vampires talk like that. She's from Europe somewhere, and her accent never left her. And although she's blunt and can come across as a bit of a bitch, she knows her shit.

And the best part is that she's always in Vegas—just our luck.

"Where is this witch?" Rachel asks.

"The Dark Hall," I say.

Rachel gives me a stupid look that says, *Is that supposed to be a funny joke?*

Drax leans into her. "It's a casino."

"How do you know she'll be there?" Rachel asks.

"She's always there," I say. "She does tarot readings for people. Charges an arm and a leg, but she's famous around here."

I glance up at Veerka, who hasn't said a word over the last few minutes. I know why she's being quiet—she knows she can't stick around and is trying to figure out how to say goodbye.

"When will I see you again?" I ask.

She smirks. "Perhaps when all of this is over."

"What?" I say. "All you've given me is a name. What the hell am I supposed to do with that? I thought we were partners."

Drax wrinkles his nose. "Partners?"

The guy must think I've lost my mind. I don't partner up with anyone... ever. He once called me his partner in crime and I punched him in the face. Getting close to people isn't my thing—I'm immortal; it's too complicated. And teaming up with a vampire? Now that's ludicrous.

But as afraid as I am of getting close to Veerka again, I can't seem to help myself. There's something so damn magnetic about her.

Ignoring Drax, I turn to Rachel. "Think you can create another portal?"

She gives me big eyes and a slack jaw—a look that I assume means, *Are you kidding me? After what just happened?*

"We need to get Veerka back to San Halos, Rachel. Lucius—" I stop, realizing Rachel knows nothing about the vampire hierarchy. "Her boyfriend's the vampire in charge of San Halos, which means he's powerful and has plenty of vampires willing to do anything for him."

"Like break into your apartment looking for you two? And what do you mean, her boyfriend? Aren't you two lesbians?"

What the fuck? Where's that coming from? I give Veerka a side-glance but don't say anything. Is it that obvious that something's going on between us?

"Would you make her the damn portal?" I say.

Rachel raises two hands on either side of her face. "Geez, okay. I assume you're going back to the hotel? I already have that location—"

"Yeah," I cut her off.

I'm not sure where my anger's coming from. Maybe it's because Veerka's leaving, I have no idea when I'll see her again, and she's going back to her fucking boyfriend.

My teeth squeak as I clench my jaw.

Rachel reaches into a little pouch at her side, pulls out a pinch of powder, and starts talking gibberish again. Riskus does the same as Rachel extracts her wand and together, they recite some incoherent lines.

She twirls her wand in a circular motion, and a blue light spits out from the tip.

Well, that's new.

How much has she been practicing over the last week? The thought is a bit frightening. It means she's been dabbling with the magic from the *Book of Origin*. She summoned a goddamn griffin, for crying out loud. What the fuck else did she unleash into the world?

It still blows my mind that this kid has the *Book of Origin*. What was I thinking? I was so selfish in wanting my money from Jamieson that I downplayed the severity of the situation.

I should have left it in my chest where it was safe. Not only will Jamieson and Lucius now hunt for it, but I'm thinking it has made its existence known to countless shadow dwellers.

As Rachel twirls her wand in the air, a large oval shape takes form. She glances back at me, and then at Veerka. "It's ready. It'll take you right outside of the Lotus Hotel, in the back alley."

When Veerka steps toward her, I can't help but

open my big mouth. "Wait."

She turns back, a foreign sadness in her eyes. This whole time, I thought vampires had no feelings—that they were nothing but predatory, empty shells. Veerka is still the same person I knew, but a lot paler and more badass.

I walk toward her, and although I want to grab her by the neck and kiss her, I don't. Instead, I extract my wrist blade and cut three lines in her dress.

"Alexis!" she shouts.

"Relax," I say, tugging at the holes. They rip wide, one of them tearing beneath her right breast. With my fingers still wrapped around the torn fabric of her clothes, I can't help but stare.

Her skin is so smooth... so soft-looking that I'm drawn back to last night. I replay everything in my mind, taking in every inch of her naked body as she begs me for more.

Drax clears his throat, pulling me out of my fantasy.

I stiffen and force an uncomfortable smile. "Um... There, that's better."

Veerka wrinkles her nose and points at her ruined dress. "How is this any better? You've made me look homeless, Alexis!"

"They can't suspect you ran away," I say. "Tell them you were kidnapped for your necklace."

She rolls her eyes the way she always does when she thinks I'm being overdramatic. "I've been with you for a week, Alexis. Why on Earth would anyone kidnap someone to steal jewelry? My kidnapper could have tied me up and taken the necklace without kidnapping me for so long. I mean, that sounds preposterous."

Tie you up... Yeah, I'll tie you up, all right. I'll tear the rest of that dress off, too, then strap you to a bed. Then, I'll—

"Alexis," Veerka says sharply.

I clear my throat. "Okay. Tell them I took you hostage for information, and you refused to give me anything. Then, the second you had the chance, you attacked me and ran away."

Her stunning smile returns. "Don't worry about me, Alexis. I'll know how to handle Lucius."

Yeah, I bet she does, which is why I hate that she's going back.

Fighting the urge to make some immature remark about how I'm better in bed, I ball my fists. "All right, go. I'll find *whatsherface* and go from there."

Veerka looks a bit concerned. "You do remember her name, don't you?"

"Yeah, yeah, go."

I'm playing it off cool, but inside, I feel like I'm being torn apart. This is why I don't let myself care for anyone. I go fucking insane. I don't know when I'll see her again, and all I can think about is that piece of shit Lucius putting his nasty hands on her.

Will she be okay?

She reaches for my face, her fingernails tickling my cheek. "See you soon, darling."

And with that, she walks into the portal and disappears.

CHAPTER 5

"Holy crap," Rachel says. She clutches hard at her *Book of Origin* and gazes around the hotel room, mesmerized.

Yeah, it's luxury. This is what happens when you stay at the Dark Hall. You pay an arm and a leg, but you're protected from virtually everything.

"So, there are no humans here?" she asks.

Reaching into the oversized fridge, I pluck out a cold beer. "No."

"How do you know it's safe?"

"This whole place is enchanted, Rachel. Feebles don't know about it. They can't see it. And the whole point of having a shadow dweller-only casino is to encourage different species to get along. The most powerful beings of all time put this place together, so you can bet your ass nothing bad happens here. They have a zero-violence policy. No conflict at all. And apparently, anyone who has exhibited violence of any type gets cursed to a hell-like dimension for eternity."

Rachel swallows so hard I hear the gulp.

"Yeah," I say. "They don't fuck around. When I tell you that your book's safe here, it is. But this isn't a permanent solution. We need to find Zerachu."

Rachel covers her mouth and giggles.

I don't even bother telling her she's being immature, laughing at some woman's name. She can have her laugh. Whatever.

Drax walks around, looking like a kid himself. Every time he finds some electronic gadget, or some fancy decoration, he points at it and turns to me with a grin.

I get it.

This place is to die for.

I walk across the room's marble floors, taking in the massive Jacuzzi, the eighty-inch television, and the ginormous windows that open up with a simple voice command. This place is even more luxurious than the Bellagio, but it's also ten times the price.

Two grand per night.

Good thing I'm a multimillionaire now.

With my beer in one hand, I reach for a bottle of Patrón on the liquor rack, open it with my teeth, and chug several shots' worth. Maybe if I drink enough, I'll stop focusing on Veerka.

Or maybe drinking isn't what I need. Now that I think about it, I'm fucking hungry.

"You guys stay here," I say.

"What?" Rachel says. "Where are you going?"

"To find Zerachu," I say.

"Can't I come with you?" she asks.

Drax plops himself down on the leather sofa, pulls out a rolling paper, and rolls a joint. When he catches me watching him, he says, "What? You don't need me. Go do your thing. I'll be right here." Then, he reaches for the TV's remote, turns it on, and squeals like a kid on Christmas morning when the high-definition screen lights up the room.

"I'd rather you stay here," I say, turning toward Rachel. "I'll come back to get you if I need you."

She looks bummed out.

"See that fridge?" I point to the one I pulled a beer out of. "It's an Apparitious 4000."

One of her reddish-brown eyebrows pulls up. "What's that?"

She doesn't know what it is, which should be no surprise. She's a newbie to the world of magic.

"Think of it as the magic genie of foods."

"Holy shit," Drax says, almost as if only tuning into my voice now. "Is that an Apparitious 4000? I thought those things weren't even real!"

He leans forward as if on the verge of getting up, but his blunt remains his priority.

"All you have to do is think about what you want, open the fridge door, and there it is," I say.

"Like, magic?" Rachel says.

No, *like mathematics.*

"Yeah," I say.

She's a witch. Why does the idea of a magic fridge surprise her?

"You wanted a beer?" she asks, staring at the

bottle in my hand.

I shift my eyes sideways like I missed the punch line. Isn't it obvious? Why even ask me that? I always want a beer.

"Try it out. Have fun. Eat whatever you want. I'll be back," I say. Before exiting the hotel room, I turn around with a rock-hard finger pointed at her. "And don't even think about trying to get anything other than food out of that thing. You'll get an explosion of magic, and trust me, it hurts."

She gulps again as I close the door behind me.

The Dark Hall Casino is like any other casino—full of bright lights, cold air pumped with oxygen, and massive crowds of people with drunken grins plastered to their faces. Now and then, someone gets upset and smashes a fist against a poker table, which is immediately followed by, "Sorry, sorry, I didn't mean to get upset".

I've been inside the Dark Hall about five times in all of my existence. It's an awesome place, but it's so damn expensive. Think of it as a reserve for the elite.

Everyone is friendly, at least on the surface. People know better than to express their discontent. Some shadow dwellers gamble for money, but it's more typical to find people bartering for weird shit like jars of eyes, fingernails, bright gooey green stuff... You catch my drift.

As I walk through crowds of odd-looking fae, I have no desire to gamble any of my money.

What I want is to feed. Correction: what I *need* is to feed. As much as I've enjoyed my hot, steamy nights with Veerka, it hasn't satisfied my succubus side. How can I feed off the living dead? Don't get me wrong—I love it. It means we can have fun nonstop without the risk of anyone getting hurt.

But now I'm left feeling hungry. Hungry me tends to be irritable... like an explosion is lingering right beneath the surface, waiting for the right opportunity to tear someone's face off. After that comes a sense of depletion and weakness, the result of starvation.

I've reached starvation a handful of times in my entire life, and I'm not about to add to that list tonight.

I walk through the casino, releasing some of my charm. It's almost like a scent—it lures people in sexually. I don't even have to go all-out succubus for it to work, and although it isn't the same Lure I use when seducing someone, it's as powerful.

Most of the casino is made up of demons, and while demons might not satisfy me the way feebles do, I don't have a choice. Feeding off a demon is about equivalent to feeding off a feeble and stopping halfway, which is what I do anyway unless I'm on the job.

Several heads turn my way as I take long strides past a dozen red felt poker tables and toward a mahogany bar. I glide my fingers along the smooth shiny wood, climb up onto the leather stool, and lean my breasts against the hard surface.

I'm about to order myself a beer when a voice with a Texan accent enters my right ear.

"Quite the drink for a fine lady like you."

Without turning my head, I glance sideways.

A Crimmus demon.

I'm not surprised—those things are everywhere. He tips his head forward and pinches the brim of his cowboy hat. "I'm Charles. How do you do?"

How do you do?

I stare at him, analyzing every inch of his body. I have nothing against Crimmus demons, but they're all so different that I want to make sure I'm getting what I need out of this one. His skin, red as blood, hides underneath a blue and white carrot-top shirt and a pair of torn jeans. He has a prominent jawline and handsome features.

The red skin is a distinguishing feature of Crimmus demons. That's how they got their name. Something to do with the color crimson. The funny thing about Crimmus demons is that aside from their immortality, they aren't special in any way. I mean, they're strong—stronger than any feeble out there—but they don't have any other special ability. When they reach adulthood, they stop aging, but that's common with most demons.

"Give the woman some space," comes another voice.

I don't even have to look to my left to know it's a Gorton demon—I can smell it.

Gortons are everywhere in Vegas. Why? Because of their greed. I'm about to roll my eyes at him based on the stereotype that Gortons are all greedy bastards, but the moment I glance his way, my irritation goes away. He smiles at me, revealing a set of glossy white teeth surrounded by a perfectly manicured scruff. He fixes his tie, smooths his jet-black hair back, and leans his upper body against the bar. Through the cold, air-conditioned air comes the scent of crisp cologne.

This, I can work with.

"Let me know if this guy's bothering you," he says.

To my right, the Crimmus demon squeezes his beer. "Can't ya see I'm conversing with this fine lady? I suggest you get on outta here and make friends elsewhere."

The Gorton smiles at me again, ignoring the Texan demon. "Let me get you a drink."

"You deaf?" the Crimmus cuts in. "I said get outta here."

Ignoring the two aggravated demons, I flick a finger at the bartender and smirk. "I'll have a beer. Whatever you recommend."

The Gorton brushes invisible lint from his ironed black suit and sucks his teeth. "See what you did there, cowboy? You made this lovely woman order her own drink."

The Crimmus tightens his red fingers around his beer again, this time shattering the bottle. It crumbles into little brown shards across the bar top.

Should I step in and stop the altercation? Maybe. I'm still subtly broadcasting my Lure, which is why these two are about ready to tear each other's throats out. But that's what I want: intensity. It'll make my feed that much more satisfying.

With blood pooled in his palm, the Crimmus leans forward, his face inches away from mine despite his glare being aimed at his opponent. "I ain't gonna ask you again, my friend—"

"Is there a problem here?" comes the bartender's voice. With furrowed brows, he slides me a frosted glass filled to the brim with caramel-colored beer. His eyes shoot sideways, which tells me he's on the lookout for security.

If I don't handle this now, I'll lose my meal, which means playtime is over.

I take a sip of my fizzy drink and place the glass on the bar top. Sighing, I reach into my coat pocket, extract a twenty-dollar bill, and lay it flat on the counter. "No problem here."

With that, I release my Lure and reach for the Gorton's tie. His eyes glaze over the moment my fingernails graze his chest, and I pull him in slowly, his warm whiskey breath slipping into my mouth. He licks his plush bottom lip, a sly smirk tugging at one side. As much as I want to grab his face and kiss him hard, I can't do that. If things heat up too quickly, I won't be able to stop, which means we'll end up fucking on this bar top and I'll get banned from the Dark Hall.

Anyone caught doing something wrong is banned from ever returning here or sent to Hellfire City—an underground prison for shadow dwellers which happens to be ruled by the infamous and legendary Hades. Hellfire City is the worst-case scenario, but being banned is awful, too, especially for those of us who are immortal.

So instead, I walk my fingers down his torso and under his belt until he gets excited.

All right, enough playing around.

I'm starving.

Grabbing hold of his tie again, I slip off my stool and drag him with me. With a tilt of my head, I throw my chin out at the Crimmus demon. "You. Get up and take us to your room."

Chapter 6

I move toward the hotel room's exit, feeling high as a bird. But right before exiting, I glance back at the two naked demons and wink. "Thanks for the pick-me-up, boys."

Now, I can focus.

As much as I want to find Devania Arkis, or whatever her name is, the issue with Rachel and that stupid *Book of Origin* is more important. Do I want to put an end to Lucius's reign? Of course. I also want to kill the son of a bitch because I don't want his hands going anywhere near Veerka.

But at the end of the day, what good is getting Veerka back if we're all dead?

If those book pages get into the wrong hands, we could all be done for. I still can't believe Rachel lost half the book to Lucius's goons, but there's no use dwelling on the past. I have to focus on finding Zerachu—who I now picture as a Pokémon thanks to Rachel—and ask her for help.

I can't think of a more powerful witch than her, and I know exactly where she is.

Strutting down the hotel corridor, I whistle a tune. I fucking love this feeling—it's better than doing coke and ecstasy at the same time. I'd say it's better than heroin, too, but what kind of role model would I be if I said something like that?

I form white-knuckled fists to contain the crazy amount of energy I have and make my way down to the Red Lounge. This is where Zerachu is, or at least, where she should be. She's famous around here, and everyone and their grandmother knows that if there's one person you want magical advice from, it's Zerachu. She also happens to give card readings—something I've had done once and refuse to do again.

I'd rather not rehash the whole thing, but she ended up being right, and I ended up binge-drinking for six months only to wake up on the side of the road soaked in my piss.

Classy, I know.

If I'm right, or if Zerachu's still in the business, she should be located at the back of the Red Lounge Casino, right next to the Blood Fang blackjack table. It's hard to miss, and it's the first thing I see as I maneuver my way through slot machines, poker tables, and weird betting games with slimeballs and boxes of fur.

Her tent is purple, and at the top of it is a wooden plank with a creepy symbol on it—an eye surrounded by little blue speckles. Long black drapes with celestial designs hang over the tent's opening, and through the crack is a bright green glow.

What's she doing in there? Magic? Zerachu isn't one to perform any magic out in the open. She's private, and despite how talented she is, she doesn't flaunt it. As I get closer, a young group of vampires walks across her tent, pointing and giggling. The tallest of the bunch, a scrawny guy with uneven fangs that don't seem to have settled in properly, bends forward, pokes a finger through the crack, and presses his eye up to it.

What a fucking idiot.

I'm about to blurt this out loud, but I don't even have the time.

In an instant, he disappears, and a giant flash of blue light replaces him. Around its edges are white lines that spit out like bolts of lightning. The whole thing happens so fast that it looks like a camera's flash. The moment the light disappears, he's gone.

Where he stood seconds ago is a little black kitten with cute, overhanging fangs. Its eyes bulge and its ears go flat as people start freaking out around him.

He tries to meow, but it comes out sounding more like a squeal.

One of his friends shrieks—a high-pitched noise that makes the kitten's hair stand on its back.

If I didn't know Zerachu, I'd be freaking out. Who does something like that to a teenager?

She does.

He'll be back to himself in twenty-four hours, and that'll teach him to keep his nose out of other people's business. It'll also teach anyone nearby to read the giant sign positioned in front of her tent:

If curtains are closed, KEEP OUT.

Beside the sign is a ticket-dispensing machine. Well, I say ticket-dispensing, but it doesn't dispense anything. Instead, it's a little wooden box with a yellow button that says, RESERVE MY SLOT. The wood is so old it looks like it came from the Middle Ages, and for all I know, maybe it did.

I've pressed this button before, so it doesn't come as a surprise when a cloudy blue digit appears on the back of my hand: 69.

I'm about to deliver an immature joke to an old demon with silver hair as she walks by me, but she's frowning so hard you'd think her face was melting. So instead, I smile to myself and glide my finger across the number.

Under the slot reservation box is cursive writing floating in the air: Now Serving 14. I roll my eyes so hard it makes a sound. "Oh, come on!"

Countless heads turn my way, but I don't care. This is fucking urgent. How am I supposed to wait for my number? What if by the time it's my turn, Lucius and his goons have already figured out how to decipher some pages from the *Book of Origin*?

"Zerachu," I say aloud.

When nothing happens, I clear my throat. "Zerachu! It's Alexis. I can't wait for my turn and I promise I'm not wasting your time."

Zerachu and I aren't best friends—I've seen her maybe a handful of times. But the few times that I have seen her, the moments were memorable, so I'm certain she remembers me, too.

Taking a step back, I squint. While I might not be touching her tent, nothing is stopping her from casting a spell from the inside. The last thing I need is to turn into a cat.

A shuffling sound comes out of her tent, followed by an irritated grunt. Out through the crack comes a hand full of rings, bracelets, and nails, and then the curtain flies open.

The moment she steps out, I blink.

The woman looks the same as she did four years ago—long scraggly blond hair that hangs over her shoulders and down her back, emerald green eyes surrounded by hundreds of thick black eyelashes, and a twisted frown that translates to, *This had better be important.*

"What happens after?" comes a shrill voice.

Zerachu rolls her intimidating eyes. "You find out after."

Every time she speaks, I can't help but feel the size of a pea. It might have something to do with her thick Russian accent, or maybe it's that Zerachu has been around for thousands of years—even longer than I have. Her history is impressive, especially the part about having worked for Dracula. Few people can say something like that without lying.

Demon history is like religion these days—there's always been conflict and war between different groups, and there are always some exceptions who don't believe differences should interfere with friendships or work collaborations.

What most people don't know, however, is that countless religious wars stemmed from underground conflicts between fae, vampires, and witches.

It was all hush-hush back then, and it still is.

"B-b-but you can't. You can't tell me something like that—"

A scrawny, middle-aged man comes stumbling out of Zerachu's tent. Thin, frail-looking glasses hang on the bridge of his nose, and an unkempt goatee covers the lower half of his face. His shoulders, sharp and bony, make me think that perhaps he has a set of wings hiding under there.

I sniff the air, catching the scent of dandelion and raw meat.

Yep, a Strikken Lussar. Whoever came up with that name must have been smoking crack, but then again, hundreds of fae names make you feel drunk when you say them aloud (I shouldn't make statements like that seeing as I'm almost always drunk).

Strikkens are known for being two-faced—literally—and having serious anger problems. On one side (the side I'm looking at), they're weak, pathetic, and whiney. That's the side people refer to as the Strikken. When they get angry, though, the Lussar makes an appearance. Admittedly, it's freaky to see, which is why most people try to talk Strikkens down when they get worked up, otherwise—

"Why are you ignoring me?" the Strikken says, his hands now shaking.

Zerachu gives me a bored look with flat eyelids—a look that tells me she isn't in the mood to deal with a Strikken's mood problems. If she were anyone else, I'd fear for her life, but that woman can handle any bullshit thrown her way.

She lets out a heavy sigh and flicks a wrist in the air. "Like I told you, come back later and I finish reading for you."

But the Strikken keeps at it. "I don't want—"

His body convulses, and in a split second, he turns around like he's about to reenter her tent. The back of his head, where you'd expect to find hair, is a face with closed eyes, tight gray lips, and scaly blue skin. Everyone nearby takes a step back; they all know what's about to happen.

In seconds, the face on the back of his head wakes up. Its highlighter-yellow eyes pop open, and the second it looks at Zerachu, the Lussar frowns so menacingly it looks like its hairless brows are going to crush the bridge of his nose.

That's not even the freaky part.

What's disturbing is how his arms and legs

reverse positions, making his back now his chest, and his ass now his crotch. Bones snap and ligaments tear. It happens so fast that it sounds like someone stepping on Bubble Wrap.

Without warning, he extracts his two-inch claws and lunges straight at Zerachu.

Several people nearby shriek and scatter, but Zerachu isn't having it. Without so much as blinking, she clicks her fingers and the Lussar explodes into rainbow-colored Christmas tinsel.

Squeals and gasps spread throughout the casino, and a crowd of horned demons wearing security uniforms rush toward the scene, their triangular red eyes darting from side to side. They have no idea what's going on—all they know is that people are freaking out.

When they see her, however, they stiffen their postures and clear their throats. The bulkiest of the group presses a button on his radio. "Cleanup in section D. I repeat: cleanup in section D."

Barely making eye contact with the witch, he adds, "I hope he wasn't too much trouble."

Zerachu rolls her eyes and jerks her chin out at me. "This had better be good."

Without saying a word, I follow her as she raises the bottom of her long mauve and forest green dress over the Lussar's tinsel remains. She doesn't even seem bothered that everyone's staring at her like she's a monster. I bet she does this all the time, and everyone knows not to get involved.

"He'll bounce back soon," she says, glancing sideways at me. "Dey alvays do."

What she doesn't mention is that despite her being the one to attack him with magic, he'll be the one banned from the Dark Hall.

As we enter her tent, two diminutive men with ball caps and long green tails come scurrying toward the pile of tinsel with brooms in their hands.

I can only assume this tinsel will be put in a holding cell until the Lussar comes back to life. What if they drop tinsel on the way there? What if that one tinsel happens to be the dude's—

"Sit," Zerachu orders.

I do as she's told me and slide the metal-framed chair toward me. On her black wooden table are cards laid out sporadically, one of which has a figure of Death on it. Most people freak out over this, but it isn't always a bad thing. All the best outcomes I've ever had have come from the Death card. It's the card with the clown face that's giving me the heebie-jeebies.

The second she sits down, she drops her wrists on the table, ticks her nails against the wood, and makes her eyes go big.

She doesn't have to say anything for me to know that means I'd better start talking.

"*Book of Origin*," I blurt.

She pulls her face back, rolls forming around her jawline.

This caught her attention. "I-I have it," I say.

I'm not the type of person who gets intimidated—not after several hundred years of being on this planet. But Zerachu... she's something different. There's an ice-cold look in her eyes that makes you feel like she could send you straight to hell with a click of her fingers. And in all fairness, the woman isn't even mean—her intentions are good, but she lacks interpersonal skills, which might have something to do with her spending countless years living in a shack.

"Vat do you mean, *you have it?*"

The last few words come out like she's spitting them at me.

"Well, *I* don't," I correct. "There's this witch—"

"A witch has the book?"

I can't tell if she's interested or downright pissed off.

"Listen, it's complicated. The kid's name is Rachel—"

"A *kid?*"

I can't tell if she's shocked or pissed off.

"It was her grandmother's, and she passed. I didn't think it was that big of a deal to give it back to her—"

"You didn't *think?*"

Okay, she's pissed.

I knew this was coming.

Throwing her hands over her head, she bursts out laughing. It isn't a laugh that tells me she's having fun; it's the kind of laugh that tells me if she doesn't let it out, something else might come out in its place.

I'd much prefer the creepy laughter over sparks and spells.

"Were you drunk again, Alexis? Is dat vut happened?"

She narrows her glowing green eyes on me, and I swallow hard. So she *does* remember who I am.

"I fucked up, okay?" I say.

She drops her hands back onto the table, sending several cards swooping through the air, and lets out a long breath through flared nostrils. Then, digging her nails into the wood, she closes her eyes.

"Vhere's da book now?"

"Which half?" I say.

Her nails dig so hard the table splits in half.

Holy shit.

"Vhich half?" She cocks an eyebrow like she's trying to look at me through a magnifying glass. "Vhich half?" she repeats, this time, her voice jumping an octave. "Do you have any idea how dangerous dat book is?"

"Yeah, I do—"

"And how did a child get ahold of zis book?" she says.

The lit candle between the two of us blows out.

Okay, she's *definitely* pissed.

"It was her grandmother's—"

All the anger on her face vanishes and she slaps

a hand over her mouth. "Celeste."

Is that supposed to mean something to me? I don't know shit about astronomy.

"I—I knew it," she breathes. "It vasn't a dream."

"What're you talking about?" I ask.

For the first time, Zerachu's face softens. She reaches for her lip, then extends her arm into the air. What the hell is she doing? She brings her arm back down, closes her eyes, and kisses her fingers.

When she doesn't respond, I clear my throat.

"I couldn't confirm because of zhe spells she cast," she says.

"What spells?" I ask.

I'm guessing Celeste is a person. Or, more specifically, Rachel's grandmother. But why is Zerachu acting so heartbroken over it? Were they friends?

"Celeste cast cloaking spells to protect zhe book," she says, "to conceal herself and her family from all shadow dwellers."

I'm about to ask her what the game plan is. Sure, it's sad. The woman's dead, but we aren't. At least not yet. And the longer we sit around here mourning someone who isn't coming back, the more time we're wasting. I'm prepared to tell her to speed things up a bit, but Zerachu's face changes abruptly, and I'm left speechless.

Her cracked bottom lip quivers and her eyes water.

She reaches for the crystal pendant around her

neck and raises it to her lips. "Rest in love and light, my dear sister."

CHAPTER 7

"My great-aunt?" Rachel blurts out.

She's so loud about it that Drax flinches, sending the TV's remote hurling through the air.

"This... this is amazing," she says, now pacing across the hotel room. "I mean, didn't you say she's the most powerful witch, like, ever? And how do I have a great-aunt? Grandma never talked about having a sister."

It's hard to feel happy about Rachel's discovery after the verbal beating I received.

"The Great Witch wants you to go see her at midnight," I say coldly.

"To train me?" she asks.

I've never seen Rachel this happy about anything before. Cracking open a bottle of beer, I shrug with one shoulder. "Something like that."

Although Zerachu agreed to coach Rachel on her magical abilities, the real reason she wants to see her is to get an understanding of what happened and to secure the book. As it turns out, Celeste—Rachel's grandmother—cast a protective spell so powerful around the book and her home that no one could determine the book's location for centuries.

I'm the idiot who came along and removed it from their home.

I don't bother going into detail with Rachel about her grandmother's real age, because it's irrelevant. One thing matters—how fast the book's protection spell is fading. Zerachu described it as a bit like an onion inside a coconut—the magic itself, or the onion, has layers upon layers, while the exterior shell protects the bulk of it.

The combination of Celeste's death and my removal of the book from their protected home was equivalent to destroying the coconut shell altogether. All that's left now are layers, and with every passing day, the magic wears off. Unfortunately for Rachel—and for all of us—those layers were damaged even more when Lucius's goons came looking for me, inadvertently causing Rachel to freak out, summon a griffin, and get the book torn in half.

"Is only a matter of days before zhe entire earthly dimension comes searching for da book," Zerachu told me moments ago.

At midnight, it's imperative that Rachel gets her ass down to the Red Lounge to meet her great-aunt.

"Bring your *half* book with you," I tell Rachel.

"Is that safe?" she asks, clutching it tight against

her chest.

"If Zerachu's involved, yes, it's safe." I chug my beer in one shot and crack open another. "She'd take it from you if she could, but she can't. Your grandma's spell somehow connected it to her bloodline. Well, her descendant bloodline, anyway. So that means you."

"Well, it would have been my mom if she had any interest in magic," Rachel says.

"Does she even know you do magic?" I ask.

She shakes her head. "I'm careful to hide it from her."

"If you're so careful," I say, "then how the hell are you all the way out here in Vegas? You're telling me your mom hasn't realized you're gone? And what about school?"

Behind her, Riskus lets out a loud squeal, jumps up on the couch, and smacks Drax with a cushion. Drax raises his arms to protect himself, but Riskus keeps beating on him.

I cock an eyebrow.

"Riskus doesn't like it when people change the channel," Rachel says.

"Would you chill?" Drax says, now trying to shoulder the little demon off of him.

Rachel lets out a sharp whistle and Riskus stops his cushion swinging midair, his back rounded and his eyes so bulged he looks like an amphibian. Grumbling something, he slouches, crosses his bony arms, and plops himself down beside Drax.

"And how the hell has your mom never seen *him*?" I add.

"Like I said," Rachel says. "I'm careful. He always hides. And besides, I took precautions before I left."

The smirk on her face tells me she played with magic again.

I can't help but glare at her. "What did you do?"

She shrugs like she's hiding some big secret, but it's obvious she's proud of whatever it is she's done. "I cloned myself."

My jaw drops and Riskus claps like he's at a New York City Broadway show.

"It worked!" he squeals. "Worked well!"

"You're telling me..." I pause because the idea is so insane that I have to let it sink in. "You're telling me you have a lookalike walking around to hide the fact that you're not home?"

Still grinning, Rachel nods. "It took fourteen tries, but I finally got it right."

I'm not sure whether to praise her or slap her. The girl plays with magic spells like they're nothing more than cool party tricks. I've seen a lot of magic mishaps, and some of that shit can't be undone.

"And is this clone physical, or is it a projection—" Realizing this can't wait, I wave a hand in front of my face. "You know what, never mind. It doesn't matter. Go see Zerachu and she'll give you all the shit you need."

"I thought you said she was my great-aunt. Why would she give me shit?"

I snort. "You haven't met the witch."

She gives me a disgusted look that tells me she's unconvinced a long-lost family member could be mean to her. We'll see. Or at least, she will.

Turning away, I toss my empty beer bottle onto one of the couch cushions. "Riskus, clean up my empties."

Rachel's brows almost touch each other. "He isn't your slave—"

"I'm paying for this room, so I make the rules. Everyone in here has to contribute, and I say Riskus is responsible for cleaning up my empties."

Rachel's about to protest, so I grab my new leather jacket I stole from a blackjack table, step out, and slam the door shut.

As much as I'd love to be a fly on the wall when Rachel meets her great-aunt, I have something else to do—I need to find Devania. It's doubtful she's in Vegas, so I might need to make friends around here to gather intel. If she's running an underground rebellion, she won't be easy to find.

With my head held high, I make my way back down to the Red Lounge.

Demons, witches, and vampires walk around like they've been friends for centuries. It's the strangest thing to see, considering the different species have been at war since the dawn of time. What I like most about the Dark Hall is that pricks like Lucius aren't welcome.

It isn't because the dude's in charge of San

Halos. The reason he's not allowed inside the Dark Hall is that everyone knows how he feels about interspecies friendships—he finds the whole notion appalling. The Dark Hall is like the Switzerland of the world. Everyone wants the same thing—to forget the hatred and corruption in the real world.

If I didn't have such a problem with managing my money, and if the Dark Hall's management team hadn't set a new rule in 1872 disallowing people from staying for more than two weeks, I'd probably spend my life living inside the Dark Hall.

Back then, I didn't understand why they'd set this rule, but now I do. Too many people were trying to escape their realities by disappearing into the Hall, and while it might have been enjoyable to forget about the magical world's monstrosities, turning a blind eye doesn't prevent wars from happening.

Out of nowhere, someone bumps into me so hard that I have to suck in a lungful of air to get rid of the colorful specks in front of my eyes.

"Oh, thoot. I'm tho thorry," says the fat vampire. He smiles from ear to ear, something I'm not used to seeing a vampire do, and rests two chubby hands on my shoulders. "Are you okay, mith? Can I get you anything? I-I-I can be tho clumthy thometimes."

The guy's so huge that I can't see anything on either side of him. Still a little dazed, I rub my forehead and blink hard. "Um, no, I'm good."

He smiles again, his eyes forming little black

moons, and squeezes my shoulder. I feel something crack and I pull away. It's like he's oblivious to how strong he is.

He turns around, a huge waddle in his step, and people clear the way as he moves.

Finally, the lights in front of me fade. "Wait!"

He stops walking, his last step coming down so heavily that the slot machine nearest to him trembles and the horned woman playing it jumps off her seat, her wild eyes darting from side to side.

"Did you thay thomething, mith?"

"Um, yeah," I say, moving in an awkward fashion toward him. Everyone's staring at us, and I realize he probably isn't the first person I should be asking, but he seems like a nice guy, so it's worth a shot. "Do you like spiders?"

He pulls his upper lip over his fangs, revealing a gummy grimace.

Obviously, it's a *no*.

"Not even... a black widow?" I say.

He's still staring at me as if I offered him a bowl of fresh vomit.

I click my fingers and point at him. "Thank you for participating in my private study, buddy."

I'm about to turn away when he lets out a thunderous laugh. "Oh, wow. A thtudy? I've never partithipated in a thtudy before! Do I get thome kind of partithipathion throphy?"

I fight the urge to slap my forehead. Great. Now everyone's watching us closely.

Flicking my wrist, I force an exaggerated smile. "Oh, no, honey, it's nothing like that. It's for my daughter's science project at school."

He looks disappointed. Without giving him the time to say anything else, I swing around, my smile disappearing and my eyes rolling up into my head.

"Thomething about thpiders," I hear behind me. "A thience project or thomething."

Goddamn it. I should've kept my mouth shut. I might be a great hit woman, but I sure as hell suck being a detective when I don't know what I'm looking for. All I can do is hope he doesn't go around talking about black widow spiders. The whole point of using that term was to be discreet, and this Michelin Man vampire looks to be anything but discreet.

Trying to hide my face, I walk fast with my head bowed. If I can at least get out of Red Lounge, I can sneak into a different casino and start over.

"Drink?" comes a young woman's voice.

I almost bump into her tray of shot glasses but stop myself in time, the tray hovering inches away from my lips.

With my head still bowed, I stare at the woman's apron—a velvet red fabric that wraps around what appears to be her naked body. Her legs, thin and toned, make me want to sink my teeth into them. On either side of the apron, the skin of her bare and perfectly round breasts peaks out, taunting me.

I know I just fed, but I'm always hungry.

Finally, my gaze reaches her face, and I can't look away. The woman's gorgeous—model material gorgeous. Her plump red lips curve at one end and she points her eyes at the shot glasses. "They're free."

Biting my lower lip, I reach for a glass, tilt it back, and swallow the burning liquid. She has no clue about what's going on—I'm bringing out my Lure.

"Is there a limit?" I ask.

She lowers her gaze to my lips. "I don't limit anything... I like to think I'm pretty adventurous."

Got her.

"I'm all about adventure," I say. "What's the point in life if you can't play?"

Her right brow pops up and she licks her lips. "I love playing. Especially with toys."

A vivid image flashes in my mind and a throbbing heat radiates between my legs. I have to bite the inside of my cheek to prevent grabbing her by the hair and dragging her into the nearest closet.

She reaches for one of her drinks, winks at me, and chugs it back.

I grin. "Why don't you show me where your room—"

"E-e-excuse me."

My eyes go huge. Who the fuck is interrupting this intense, heated moment?

Begrudgingly, I turn toward the voice to find a scrawny man with a major slouch in his posture. He wears Coke-bottle glasses that make his black eyes look five times their regular size. His skin, a light—almost white—beige, matches his short, unkempt hair, which looks like it's been combed forward, causing long, uneven points to hover above his brows. His head twitches from side to side as he stands there, and I can't tell if he's nervous or if he has a tic.

I say nothing—I think the look on my face says it all: *What the fuck do you want?*

"I-I-I heard you're looking for... for a spider."

Goddamn it. What kind of freak did I attract?

"I'll give you two a moment," the woman says, giving the strange little man a full up-and-down look.

"No," I blurt, but she turns away, having clearly lost all interest.

No shit. This guy threw me off my game and fucked up my Lure.

Clenching my fists, I breathe out hard, his body almost disappearing as I narrow my eyes.

"Or a black... widow?" he says eerily, his big bug eyes darting from left to right.

Is this guy for real? How could someone like him know anything about an underground rebellion? He looks like someone who used to be a mouse in his past life.

And wow. When did I become so judgmental?

I guess being a thousand years old does that to a person.

"You know about black widows?" I ask.

He scrunches his nose and pulls his upper teeth back to reveal two long yellow front teeth, then nods so fast it looks like another one of his twitches.

A Ratiken demon—of course. And yes, the name is derived from the rodent. These demons are known to look terrified all the time. You sneeze and they squeal. But Ratikens have proven themselves useful for transmitting messages to people across the globe. They're rats, after all. They travel underground, in the sewers, in ventilation systems... anywhere they can to collect information. Why? Because information pays.

"Tell me what you know," I say.

He searches the room behind me again and sways his head from side to side, his oversized ears moving in all directions as he takes in the noise around us.

I've been so busy analyzing his giant eyes that I didn't even notice those satellites for ears, which are always a clear indication of this demon's race. Those, and—

With hands hanging in front of his chest like raptor arms, he swings around, and a giant hairless tail sweeps the floor.

Yeah, that.

"Come on," he says in a sharp whisper. "I'll show you."

CHAPTER 8

"I-I-I'm Peter, by the way," says the Ratiken.

He takes me across the Red Lounge and toward the bathroom corridor. I'd be lying if I said I wasn't a bit reluctant to follow a Ratiken into a bathroom. I'm told they have some magical abilities, and for all I know, he's capable of flushing me down a toilet and sending me to his sewer friends.

We walk down the corridor, passing a male witch and a short hairy demon, and Peter stops in front of a solid steel door that reads, *Staff Only*.

He makes a weird ticking sound with his mouth, like he's clicking his teeth together, and reaches into his shirt. Out comes an access card hanging on a lanyard, and with it, he swipes the small electronic box next to the door's handle.

A soft beep comes from the machine, followed by the clicking sound of something unlocking.

Pushing the door open, he jerks his head sideways, signaling me to follow.

I can't help but glance down both ends of the corridor before going in. While I don't often give a shit about rules or the law, I'd be lying if I said I wasn't afraid of getting banned from this place or getting sent to Hellfire City.

But I need to find Devania, so I suck in a sharp breath and follow Peter the Ratiken inside the staff room.

To my surprise, no one else is inside. Overhead, the lights are dim, almost like the power's gone out and the hotel's being run off a backup generator. One light keeps flickering, making me want to expand one of my wings and smash it with my claw.

It's creepy as fuck.

Biting my tongue, I do my best to ignore it. Peter leads me through what appears to be a staff kitchen—again, completely empty—and I follow him through another door. There's something off about this one. It looks like something taken off a castle centuries ago with its orange, wet-looking wood. Running horizontally across the panels are two slabs of black iron, and next to one of them is a long handle made of the same material.

What the hell is something like *that* doing in a modern kitchen like *this*?

Turning sideways, he aims one of his black beady eyes at me. "Can you see it?"

I crinkle my nose. "See what? The door?"

He pulls his lips over his big front teeth and nods. "Good."

Who the fuck would miss something like that? I squint at it when I realize there's moss on the damn thing. And it's not like this door is limited to magical eyes only—it's sitting in the goddamn Dark Hall. Most people here have some sort of magical ability.

He reaches for the handle, and when the door doesn't open, he brings in his other hand and hops up and down. His face turns beet red, and a squiggly vein pops out on his left temple.

"You need help?" I ask.

"It's… it's jammed."

I fight the urge to smile. I doubt it's jammed—the guy looks like he'd strain a muscle trying to lift a twig.

He hops hard one last time, using his tail to hold him up, and a loud clicking sound fills the air. Glancing into the kitchen with his mouth wide open, he nods fast. "Okay, hurry."

I can't see anything behind the door; it's pitch black. He wants me to go in there? Whatever. What choice do I have? My succubus eyes will adjust. I step inside, and he shuffles behind me. His breath is short and fast as if he finished running a marathon moments ago or suffers from a deviated septum.

Or maybe both.

To be honest, it's irritating. I hate the sound of heavy breathing unless I'm the cause of it.

I'm tempted to tell him to shut up, but I don't have the time. Behind us, the massive door slams shut and I flinch. I blink hard to bring my succubus eyesight into play, but it doesn't work.

I can't see shit.

"Where are we?" I hiss.

"Where do you want to be?"

Now he's asking for it.

"What's your problem?" I say. "I'm not in the mood to play mind games."

He must sense that I'm about to deck him. I might not be able to see him, but I know where's he's standing and with those big ears of his, it wouldn't be difficult to get a good grip on my target.

"You're in the Hall of Hollows," he says like it's some big secret.

"Is that supposed to mean something?"

"You've never heard of it?" he asks.

I grind my teeth so hard they squeak. Who leads someone into some weird-ass place with the assumption that they already know about it? What he should have done was explain everything to me before we set foot inside this Hall of Whatevers.

"It's a creation ground," he says.

"Explain faster," I order.

"All you have to do is put forth an intention of where you want to go."

"So basically, you're telling me I can teleport anywhere."

"Technically speaking, it isn't teleportation—"

Although I can't see him, I can picture his big teeth moving up and down over his lower lip. It might have something to do with the fact that I can

74

hear his massive overbite.

He continues. "I heard you were looking for—"

Impatient, I wave a hand in the air, and although I can't even see my hand, the sound of my jacket chafing must have been enough to shut him up.

"I know who I'm looking for," I say. "How do I do this? Do I picture finding her and click my shoes together three times?"

"Why would you click—" he tries.

Rolling my eyes, I let out a sharp breath. "Give me instructions."

When he doesn't respond, I snap, "Now!"

He lets out a squeal so high-pitched I reach for my ears. "Dude, what the fuck was that?"

"S-s-sorry," he says. "You startled me."

Instead of saying anything this time, I shut my mouth and wait for his instructions. At the moment, he's my one option for finding this Devania lady. The last thing I want to do is scare him away.

"With your mind, put out your intention," he says. "Imagine where you want to be, or *why* you want to be there. If the Hall of Hollows thinks you're worthy enough to continue, it'll guide you."

I'm about to make some smart-ass remark about it being impossible for space to *think*, but by now, I know that anything in this universe, and every other-dimensional version of it, is possible.

So instead, I close my eyes and my mind strays toward me kissing Veerka's bare chest, her hips, her thigh—

Shit.

Clearing my throat, I try to think about *how* I'll find my way back to Veerka. She told me to find a woman named Devania Arkis, and that this woman would be the one to help us fight the battle against vampire corruption. And the only way for me to get Veerka back is to ensure Lucius loses his reign, hence why I'm going through with this mission. The problem is I don't know what this lady looks like, or where she might be, but what I know most of all is that I *need* to find her.

The blackness around me turns into a bright white light, and I turn in time to see Peter smiling up at me, his slimy front teeth looking even more yellow than I remembered underneath this blinding light.

"Good luck with the trial," he says.

"Trial? What the f—" I don't have time to finish. At once, the light disappears, and I'm standing in what looks like an abandoned warehouse.

I turn toward Peter again, but he's gone.

Great. Fucking great.

"Yeah, right there," someone says.

I swing the other way but realize this warehouse-looking place is full of people. Most of them look like witches from centuries ago—pointed hats, long suede cloaks, staffs, and spell books under their noses.

What's going on? I intended to find Devania—

the leader of the underground rebellion. Why are there witches here? And fae? I assumed the rebellion would be made up of vampires. Maybe I have this all wrong. I'm *assuming* Devania is a vampire, when she might be something else entirely.

I wish I could teleport back to where I was and strangle Peter for giving me such shitty instructions.

I move forward, the wooden floorboards under my feet creaking, and observe everyone around me. They're all hunched over old-looking tables like they're playing scratch cards. Why are they so focused? Two young witches with matching red pigtails say something aloud and pour a jarful of green slime into a cauldron. They turn around and block their ears like they're anticipating an explosion. When nothing happens, they grin from ear to ear and high-five each other.

Then, a short male witch brushes past me.

"Um, excuse me," I try.

He's either deaf, or he doesn't care. He doesn't even bother turning around to look at me, and instead, smacks his forehead as if trying to remember something from his childhood.

"Okay," I mutter.

When another witch walks by me, I extend my hand to touch her shoulder. But she halts before I make contact, bites her bottom lip, and spins around so fast I don't even have time to say anything.

What are they all working on? It's like they're trying to solve the mystery of life. No one even realizes I'm standing here. Can they not see me?

"Hello?" I say, my voice growing louder.

Nothing.

Seriously? Am I invisible? It wouldn't be the first time that happened.

"Are you all blind?" I shout.

At once, everyone stops what they're doing, and dozens of eyes roll my way.

Okay, they *can* see me.

"Did you hear that?" asks one of the red-pigtailed witches.

She's staring through me and at the door at the front of the warehouse.

Are you fucking kidding me?

Is this what Peter was talking about when he said it wasn't technically teleportation? Is that because I'm not actually here?

"Hello?" I shout.

The way they keep turning their heads, it's obvious they can hear something.

"Probably another Searcher," one woman whispers.

A Searcher? What the hell's that supposed to mean? Breathing in a long, calculated breath, I close my eyes. I'm here for a reason, and all I have to do now is figure out what it is. Peter said something about being worthy. If I mouth off and throw shit, I don't think I'll pass whatever this *trial* is.

"Miss Rayne?" comes a deep voice from behind me.

I twirl around so fast my stolen leather jacket slaps itself.

The man standing before me isn't the type of person I'd expect to see in a place like this. He smiles at me, or at least, he tries to and reveals two pointed fangs at the corners of his lips. His face is white as snow, the same as his perfectly combed hair. The two combined make his entire head look like a glow-in-the-dark ball in this dim space.

"You can see me?" I say.

Still smiling, he offers a slow nod like he's amused. I don't see what's funny about any of this.

"Where am I?" I ask.

"I believe you were already given instructions on how to proceed."

The words come out with an ancient Old English accent, and for a second, it almost makes me forget how much I fucking hate it when people don't answer my questions. It isn't rocket science. Someone asks a question and you answer it. And what came out of his mouth has nothing to do with my question.

"Where am I?" I repeat, my tone hardening.

I'm not sure if I'm pissed off because he didn't answer my question, or because I wasn't given any instructions by Peter.

"That, Miss Rayne, is up to you."

Stay calm. Stay calm. Stay calm.

It sucks knowing you have anger issues and not being able to control them. I'm well aware that I'm boiling on the inside—somewhat unnecessarily—but I can't help it. I'm sobering up, I don't know what the fuck is going on, and apparently, the fate of San Halos and possibly the world lies with me.

Well, that's how Veerka made it sound, anyway. I might be blowing it up a bit in my head because I like to imagine myself as her knight in shining armor. I won't even bother turning that statement into a female version because I enjoy gender-bending.

So instead of exploding, I picture myself going down on Veerka and that seems to work.

That's the ultimate goal, isn't it? Getting to keep her as mine.

I haven't a clue who this vampire is, why he can see me, or how he knows my name, but it's obvious he has something to do with this trial I've been forced into.

"What do you want from me?" I ask.

"This is not about what I want, Miss Rayne. I believe you are searching for something."

All right, so this guy isn't a total quack. My eyes narrow on him, but he doesn't seem to mind. I'm almost tempted to use my Lure to get him to answer me, but oddly, it feels inappropriate. It's like he's some ancient guru, thousands of years old, and the idea of bringing any form of sexual energy near him would be disrespectful.

I've never felt that way before. I don't often give a shit how my Lure will affect the other person, but for some reason, I can't bring myself to do it on this vampire.

"I *am* looking for something—someone," I correct. "The Black Widow."

Slowly, he removes his hand from his belly and extends it out as if preparing to blow a handful of magic dust from his palm. Long wavy nails point outward—nails you'd think haven't been cut in over a century.

"If your heart is true, you will find her," he says.

Don't roll your eyes... Don't roll your eyes...

I haven't even started the trial and I feel like I'm failing. My heart is anything but true. Despite this, I take a step in the general direction of where he's pointing. As I move forward, the entire warehouse flickers, almost as if I'm standing inside a television and the video footage is losing its signal.

The large gathering of witches moving about like elves in Santa's Village becomes translucent, and as the crowd disappears, a long dirt trail emerges right in the middle of the warehouse.

With the words *What the fuck* prepared to slip out of my mouth, I turn back to look at the old vampire and discover he's gone.

CHAPTER 9

The translucent crowd of witches continues to move around sporadically, some walking right through me as I make my way to the dirt path.

The moment I step onto it, a cool gust of wind sweeps into me, bringing along with it the smell of pine, wet earth, and fresh lavender. Farther ahead is a thick forest masked by rising fog. I'd be lying if I said the forest looks inviting. It feels like I'm about to step onto some Halloween movie production set. Every time the wind blows, swirls of white swim through the air.

It's downright creepy.

But there's a reason this path appeared, so I have to trust that I'm doing the right thing by entering the forest.

I glance from side to side, even though no one in the warehouse can see me, and slowly make my way into the forest. The dirt path feels soft under my boots—at least softer than old planks of wood. The farther I go, the quieter everything around me becomes. The bickering witches sound like nothing more than an old radio emitting sound from across a house.

Overhead, crows sit atop dry branches, cawing every time I take a step forward. I can't tell if they're encouraging me to continue or warning me of what's to come.

Suddenly, one of them takes off, its powerful wings sending a few dead leaves spinning through the air.

You'd think that being immortal would make me immune to being jumpy. After all, what do I have to be afraid of? It's not like I can die. Well, at least not easily. Deep down, though, I don't think it's the fear of death that scares me—it's the fear of eternal suffering.

I think that's what scares most immortal beings. I mean, once you're dead, you're dead. But the idea of being imprisoned for all of eternity, or worse, tortured every day, is enough to drive someone mad.

I've heard countless stories of vampires being punished through eternal torture. While everyone's version of torture is different, vampires imprison their enemies and starve them of blood. Then, right before the prisoner is so weak they can barely move, their captor places a dropperful of blood, allowing a single droplet to fall out every hour.

Sick, right?

I've heard stories about succubi being imprisoned behind glass walls and forced to watch other people fuck.

You think your vibrator battery dying right before you get off is torturous? Or having a girl—or guy—stroke you only to turn around and say they aren't feeling well? Imagine that feeling a hundredfold.

Then amplify it another hundredfold.

I feel sick to my stomach thinking about it, so instead, I focus on the murky path ahead of me and keep walking.

How far am I supposed to walk? I can't believe Veerka put me up to this shit. It better be worth it.

I picture her naked, smiling playfully up at me from underneath a candlelight's glow. A throbbing sensation radiates down my stomach and in between my legs.

It'll be worth it.

I walk for what feels like hours. Am I going in circles? Everything looks the same: the trees are tall and slanted, fog floats around my ankles, and every few minutes, a single crow caws... And it sounds the same every single time.

What kind of sick game is this?

"Hello?" I shout.

Like in horror movies, my voice echoes over and over throughout the forest.

"What the hell do you want from me?" I shout.

The last few words echo again, moving farther and farther away from my ears.

"We want you," comes a soothing voice.

Spinning around, I spot a naked couple. The man has long luscious brown hair and glistening skin covered in black tribal tattoos. His chest is so muscular that it's rounded, and his shoulders are twice the width of the woman's. With a strand of hair dangling in front of his face, he smiles at me, then wraps his fingers around the woman's curvy hips.

Like him, her eyes are on me. She pulls her long blond hair over one shoulder, allowing it to hang over her chest.

With his veiny, muscular hands, the man bends her forward and takes her.

Holy shit.

Unable to look away, I swallow hard, my throat sticking.

They should know better than to taunt a succubus.

Grinding my teeth, I bow my head.

I'll show you how it's really done...

I'm about to charge at them when another sound captures my attention.

It's the last sound I want to hear when I'm this hungry—the sound of a frightened woman.

"Help!" she cries out.

Begrudgingly, I turn around to spot a young woman in a bright red coat and shoes to match. Her long, wavy brown hair flows behind her as she runs, a look of sheer panic on her face. With her mouth open wide, she breathes out hard to catch her breath, her cheeks reddening in the process.

What's she running from?

First, I hear it; then I see it.

The monster's footsteps send vibrations into the soles of my feet as it approaches, and then its head—well, all three heads—emerge from the forest's greenery.

It roars out, its three heads bouncing up and down as it chases the woman.

The thing looks like a Cerberus pulled right out of ancient Greece... something I've encountered once before and hoped to never encounter again. Drool spills from its three mouths as it snaps at the air with its massive canine teeth.

Holy shit.

Behind me, the naked couple keeps going at it, torturing me.

How the fuck am I supposed to decide this? The girl needs help. But she isn't even real, right? It must be some illusion to distract me from feeding. What I need is a good meal. Maybe after that, I can save her.

It's not like it'll take me long to eat.

I take a step toward the couple and their smiles widen.

"I want you," the woman breathes.

Although the man's the one having his way with her, she's talking to me.

If I don't feed now, I might implode.

"Don't you want me?" she asks, biting her lower

lip.

"Help!" comes the shrill voice again.

Goddamn it.

This is fucking bullshit.

I clench my teeth so hard my jaw pops.

Without giving myself any time to regret my decision or to think about how hungry I am, I expand my wings and launch myself toward the Cerberus.

Chapter 10

Extracting my wrist blades, I hurl through the air and straight for the Cerberus. But before I can even attempt to cut off one of its heads, the creature's shape begins to lose form and distort. Are my eyes playing tricks on me, or is he disappearing?

Gradually, a swirling green light encompasses his body, along with the woman's. Before I can comprehend what the hell is happening, the two disappear as fast as a hummingbird's wings.

Are you kidding me? I turned down feeding for what? For nothing? All of that sexual frustration needs to go somewhere, and slicing off some heads would have helped me with that.

Gritting my teeth, I land hard in a pile of leaves. Maybe the couple is still going at it. Maybe—

When I twirl around, they're still gone.

What a fucking downer.

I'm about to shout something like, *This isn't a trial, it's a tease, you sick motherfucker!*

Thankfully, I'm distracted before the words come spilling out of my mouth. The forest instantly brightens as though illuminated by ten suns. All around me, leaves turn a vivid green, the fog lifts, and countless lavender plants spring out of the forest floor. In the overhead branches, where crows were cawing minutes ago, are songbirds chirping away as if celebrating something.

How did everything go from being so dark and gloomy to peppy and cheerful?

Gross.

Up ahead appears a cloud of purple smoke that matches the lavender plants. At first, it looks like cotton candy, but as the smoke dissipates, a small wooden cabin comes bursting up from the earth, its wood cracking and snapping as it sends twigs and leaves flying in every direction.

Although it sounds like it's being demolished, by the time the cracking stops, the house looks like it's been standing there for decades.

What the hell's going on?

It doesn't take a genius to know that the cabin's where I'm supposed to go next.

Rolling my eyes, I march my way to the cabin. Though deep down, I know I should be behaving with more class, I can't shake my anger over what happened. That's like letting a drug addict lick a pill, then tucking that same pill in your pocket and laughing at them. You can't fucking do that to someone like me.

So whoever's hiding out in that cabin had better be damn well worth it.

I loosen my fists when I realize I have them clenched. While I might be pissed off, I can't come across as some psychotic bitch when I enter the place. I'm here to find Devania—a woman whose sole purpose in life is to take down corruption and evil. Punching in faces won't get me very far with her.

As I approach the cabin, the front door creaks open as if the energy of my presence alone were capable of moving inanimate objects. I wish. That'd be pretty fucking sick.

I think what it means is that whoever's inside the house is expecting me.

Moving quietly, I push the door open. "Hello?"

Nothing.

As I enter, the smell of fresh peanut butter cookies and peppermint candy fills my nostrils.

I'm beginning to think I ended up in the same forest as Hansel and Gretel. Rumor has it the witch is still alive. No one's been able to prove it, which has caused a lot of speculation. Until his death, however, Hansel swore up and down he watched her burn to ashes.

I've never been convinced. Everyone knows witches have sneaky ways around shit.

But as I inhale the warm, succulent fumes, I can't help but feel like I'm being lured into something.

It can't be as bad as what I just went through. Sure, I like food as much as the next girl, but I could never be seduced by it.

"Hello?" I repeat.

A floorboard creaks and I extract my wrist blades on instinct.

"H–h–hello," comes a mousy voice.

Out from the darkness of the candlelit space comes a small woman with a tight gray bun atop her head, a rounded back, and a silver robe that drags behind her bare, veiny feet. In her right hand is an oil lantern casting a bright yellow light toward me. It rattles as she walks, and I can't tell if it's due to trembling legs or trembling hands. Her left hand—or at least what remains of it—supports the base of the lantern.

The woman's old—like, super old.

I'm surprised she's still breathing.

On her face are thick round glasses, and behind them, blue eyes with sagging lower lids. They sag so much that pink flesh hangs around her eyeball.

"Hi," I say plainly.

Who is this woman?

As she walks, her head bobbles. Is she nodding at me, or is this related to her old age? She places her lantern down on a yellow oak table, clears her throat, and slowly lowers herself onto a three-legged stool next to it.

"I've been waiting for you," she says, her voice sounding like it's being taken for a ride on a roller coaster.

"Um, hi," I say.

Her head keeps bobbing and all I want to do is grab it and hold it straight.

She sucks in a wavering breath, taps her fingers on the table, and aims her gaze at me.

Somehow, I feel compelled to sit down next to her.

Shit. Maybe she is the witch from the story. Well, I'm here now, and there's no going back. I pull out a stool and sit down.

"You acted selflessly," she says.

I stare at her. What's she talking about?

I keep expecting a smile to pull at the corner of her lips, but it's like she's too old to use those muscles.

"You have proven yourself worthy, child."

Is this about me choosing to save the woman over feeding? It's not like I was given much of a choice. And I didn't put much thought into it. The lady was screaming. If anything, she would have distracted me while I was feeding. I don't see how that makes me some hero. This lady's delusional.

Finally, her lip twitches and her big blue eyes soften. "You still do not know who you are, do you, child?"

My eyes dart around the room. Okay, what is this? Some sort of prank? The words are coming out like she's some mystical being about to tell me I'm destined to save the world.

I hold in a scoff.

"Listen," I say, cutting her off before she can

give me some cheesy speech. "I'm looking for Devania. A good friend of mine asked me to find her and told me we need her if we plan on getting rid of vampire corruption."

The old woman lowers her head to stare at me from behind her glasses. "Why do you wish to eliminate such power?"

I'm taken aback by her question. Why else would I have come all this way? Veerka asked me to, and I'll do whatever she wants if it means getting to have her as my own.

The woman must sense my reluctance to answer her question. She stiffens her back—well, as much as she physically can with that turtle posture of hers—and gazes intently at me. "You deny your heart."

I'm not denying shit. I want Veerka. I want her in every way imaginable—on her back, on her stomach, between my legs—and if I have to take down a whole fucking Vampire Mafia to get her, I'll do it.

A smirk creeps onto the woman's face, and I can't help but wonder if she can read my mind. I might want to lay off the naked thoughts until I get out of here. Otherwise, she might no longer see me as being *worthy*.

"Most living beings require several motivators to accomplish great things," she says.

I don't know what she's getting at, but I'll listen. She didn't react when I said Devania, which means she knows who she is and knows how I can find her.

"While you might believe love to be your greatest motivator, something else is shining within you."

She aims a trembling finger toward my chest. "Something destined for greatness."

Oh God...

Don't roll your eyes, don't roll your eyes, don't roll your eyes.

I'm tempted to tell her it's the sex I want, not the love, but I'll only be digging my own grave. Besides, if she *can* read my mind, she already knows what I'm thinking.

"This world has made you cold, Alexis, but the goodness within you cannot be drowned out."

My eyes widen. How does she know my name?

"I don't know what you're trying to get at," I say, getting a little impatient, "but I need to know how to find Devania. Can we please skip all this chitchat and get straight to the point?"

Without saying a word, the woman bows her head and extends a veiny hand toward a bright fireplace at the back of the cabin. The second I lay eyes on it, it makes a swooshing sound and lights up with dancing red flames.

I don't get it.

What does a fireplace have to do with Devania? Is there a secret door behind that thing? It looks large enough to be a secret doorway.

"Admit your truth, Alexis, and the flames will

lead you to where you need to go."

I'm getting sick of these fucking riddles. Clenching my jaw, I stand up, but the woman's ice-cold hand catches me by surprise.

"You cannot keep blaming yourself for the past."

Our eyes lock.

What's she talking about? How could she know anything about my past?

Using the oak table for support, she stands up, her head barely reaching my chest.

"You hide behind pain, child."

I want to pull away, but I can't. She knows things. I can't explain how, but she does. It's almost as if she's spent her entire life following me, and as I stare into her eyes, I feel at home.

What? No... I can't be. This doesn't make any sense.

"Mother?" I breathe.

One of her hairless brows pops up and she pulls her wrinkled face back.

Guess not.

Okay, that was embarrassing. Why'd she give me mixed signals like that?

And what was I thinking? She couldn't possibly by my mother—I'm not even sure why the thought popped into my head. I'm about to scold her for fucking with my emotions like that and allowing me to make a total fool of myself when she points at the fire again.

I follow her aim, and my throat swells.

Inside the flames is a vivid flash of families screaming—mothers, fathers, and children running inside a burning village. Inside *my* village.

I want to turn away, but I can't.

Instead, I watch as my younger brother screams and runs in circles as fire engulfs his little body. My parents try to help him, but it's no use. As people attempt to run from the chaos, pale faces sweep through the village, moving about so fast it's almost impossible for anyone to see them.

But now, as I watch the devastation unfold inside the fire's flames, I see them clearly.

My older sister charges toward one of them with an iron pitchfork in her grasp, but it's no use. A dark-eyed vampire swoops in, slicing her throat open with its sharp fingernails. Blood splatters inside the fireplace, and I flinch. My chest tightens as I watch my sister fall to her knees.

As I did centuries ago, I stand still, unable to move.

I want to help, but I'm too afraid.

I remember Papa teaching me how to use my wings that day, but for some reason, I couldn't extract them... I couldn't save them.

The old woman clicks her fingers and the bloody scene fades from the flames.

"You were young," she says.

Although I want to look at her, I can't. I stare at the fire, feeling like I'm about to shatter into a thousand pieces. It's one thing to think about the past repeatedly—it's quite another to relive it.

"Evil did that," she says, pointing into the fire. "Not you."

"I should have helped. I knew how to fly. I could have saved them."

The old woman shakes her head. "Your anger is destroying you, Alexis."

My throat swells so much I feel like it'll split open. I'd do anything to chug down an entire bottle of tequila right about now.

Rather than allowing myself to break down and cry, I do what I'm best at—I get angry.

"Why'd you show me that?" I snap.

"To remind you that people suffer at the hands of evil. You are no longer a child, Alexis. You can protect the vulnerable."

"Why are you even doing this? How does showing me my past help me at all? Tell me where Devania is. I'm getting fucking sick of playing this game."

She doesn't react to my anger. Instead, she smiles sweetly, bows her head, and extends that same open palm at the fire again. I'm afraid to look into it, but I can't help myself.

Thankfully, nothing happens. All I see is a fire licking logs of wood.

"What am I looking at?" I say through gritted teeth.

With her arm still extended, she says, "The

doorway."

CHAPTER 11

It takes everything in me not to laugh in her face.

She's on crack if she thinks I'm about to step foot inside a lit fireplace.

"If your heart is true, you will not burn."

"Did you pull that out of the bible, or your ass?" I say.

I feel like an asshole the second it comes out of my mouth, but it's too late to take it back. "I'm sorry," I blurt.

She doesn't seem bothered by my attitude. It's like she expects it from me.

"Who are you, really?" I ask.

She makes her eyes go big at the fireplace.

"You can't seriously expect me to walk into a fire," I say.

Is this lady insane? I might not die, but I'm not exactly in the mood to have my skin melt off. I think back to the image in the fireplace and feel sick to my stomach. No matter what this lady says, the burning of my village will always be my fault.

My parents didn't ask to find me abandoned at

the edge of the forest. They also didn't ask for a demon child. It's my fault the vampires came searching for me in the village. They got word of a demon living among feebles and wanted to put an end to it. Instead of saving the people I cared about, I ran.

I let them die.

I'm a fucking coward.

And so is my biological mother for having abandoned me in the first place.

Is she even alive? Deep down, part of me hopes so, while the other part of me hopes she rots in hell.

The old lady remains silent. I could stand around waiting for her to spill, but that may never happen. There's one thing left to do, and that's to walk into the fireplace and hope for the best. I'm tempted to ask her why we can't put the flames out before I walk in, but I know she'll give me some lame excuse about the universe requiring more of me than that.

Spirituality isn't my thing, nor is magic, so I won't overthink it. My one option is to cross my fingers and hope I don't fry.

If your heart is true, I keep hearing in my head.

My heart's true—it's fucking beating, isn't it? If this has something to do with being a good person, well, my odds aren't all that good. I've done a lot of awful shit in my life.

Sucking in a deep breath, I move toward the fire, fighting to push the thought of Veerka out of my head. Not that sex is a bad thing, but thoughts of sex and booze have been all-consuming lately.

Okay, that's a lie. It isn't only *lately*; they're *always* on my mind.

Clenching my fist, I reach out a hand and feel the fire's warmth spread across my knuckles. Don't get me wrong, I've walked through more fires than I can count, but not intentionally. And it was a quick in-and-out—something I'm not too fond of.

You aren't a bad person, Alexis. Bad shit happened to you.

I roll my eyes at my self-talk. How is it that my mind is now trying to give me some speech about being a good person? Did this lady brainwash me or something?

"Why do you want to find Devania?" comes the woman's mousy voice again.

With my fist still extended in front of me, I turn my head. Didn't I already answer this? Veerka asked me—

"Who would benefit from you finding the Black Widow?" she asks.

"A lot of people," I say. "Sons of bitches like Lucius get away with ruining lives every single day."

The words surprise me more than they appear to surprise her. Why did I even say that? I don't give a shit about other people. This world isn't my problem, and it sure as hell isn't my job to fix it. Besides, even if I wanted to, it's out of my control. The only thing I have control over is myself.

"This is your chance to fight for the greater good," she says.

I can't help it—finally, my eyes roll, and as they do, the woman reaches into the side of her cloak. From her oversized pocket, she extracts what appears to be a small doll made of straw and hemp, while its hands and feet are made of carved wood. Its left hand, however, is cut in half. From anyone else's perspective, this thing might look like some creepy ass voodoo doll from the Middle Ages.

But to me, it's the most precious thing in the world.

"Where did you get this?" I say, my words coming out as more of a bark.

She smiles at me for the first time, and I feel comforted. There's something about her eyes... I know this woman. Why won't she tell me who she is? Something catches my attention—a glimmer coming from her chest.

The fire's glow shines off of it, making it look like an icicle on a sunny winter day.

I know that necklace. It's a clear quartz pendant held together by a hemp rope. While it might sound generic, it isn't. The hemp rope is encrusted with pieces of black tourmaline—something only a witch would wear. And I've seen a necklace like this just once before.

Now, it all makes sense.

"I've been waiting a long time for you, Alexis."

* * *

"Give it back!" I shouted.

My little brother William giggled and pulled my doll away. He had his own toys. Why was he touching mine? Alice was all I had left to remind me of my real parents. As far as I know, Alice was wrapped up with me in a cotton sheet when Papa found me at the edge of the forest.

With a thudding heart, I bared my teeth. "Give it back, now!"

A grin stretched over his face, but before another laugh could come blasting out, something happened. I wasn't quite sure what it was at first. All I knew was that William looked petrified.

Quickly, Papa cleared his throat and scooped my young brother into his arms. As my father rushed him out of the room, William dropped my doll, his wide-open eyes never leaving mine.

"What's going on?" came my mother's voice.

The moment she stepped into the room, she sucked in a sharp breath and slapped both hands over her mouth.

Papa came rushing back in without William.

"Never you mind, love," he said, wrapping his arms around my mother.

With parted lips, she tried to say something, but nothing came out. Instead, she stared at me as if I were some ghost haunting their home.

"We spoke about this," he reassured her. "Do you remember?"

With hands still flat over her mouth, she nodded

quickly.

Papa kissed her cheek, rubbed her shoulder, and turned to me. Kneeling on one knee, he picked up Alice and held her flat in his palm.

"Do you remember what we spoke of, my *sweeting*?" he asked me, his voice calm and soothing.

I shook my head.

"This has to be our little secret," he said.

I wasn't sure what he was talking about until his eyes rolled up toward the ceiling and around my body. I followed his gaze to find large bat-like wings extended on either side of me.

I flinched, causing the wings to move along with me, which made me panic more.

"Do not be afraid, child," he said, his warm grasp around my shoulders. "Nothing is wrong with you."

My lower lip trembled. Nothing wrong with me? Something was terribly wrong with me. Why did I have these ugly black wings?

Smiling sweetly, he reached toward the top of my head and touched something. I couldn't tell what it was until I followed his hand and felt a sharp poke.

"You are a special creature," he said. "You have beautiful wings and beautiful horns."

He thought they were *beautiful*?

How? Every day, people in the village talked about how disgusting *horned* creatures were, along with *fanged* creatures, whatever that meant.

"The people of this village do not understand you, my dear Emily. You mustn't reveal yourself to anyone. Do you understand?"

I nodded quickly, though I wasn't sure how I was going to hide something like this from everyone in the village. What if this happened again? What if I accidentally let my wings come out?

"This doll," Papa said, reaching into his pocket, "was given to you to protect you." He pulled out his favorite carving knife and held its blade on Alice's left hand.

"What are you doing, Papa?" I shouted.

Without saying a word, he raised a solid hand, which was enough to silence me. Then, digging his blade into Alice's hand, he sliced off a small piece of wood.

I wanted to cry. How could he hurt her like that? But before I burst into tears, he reached for his boot and pulled out its suede lace.

What was he doing?

"This wood, my sweeting, was taken from the Enchanted Forest. Do you see these green markings?"

I nodded.

Wrapping the small piece of wood inside the suede lace, he smiled up at me. "It might not always be possible for you to keep this doll on you. May I?"

With a trembling lip, I extended my little arm, allowing him to fasten the bracelet around my wrist.

He'd wrapped the suede around the wood so many times I couldn't see it at all.

"Men have died trying to obtain this wood to build indestructible weapons," he said. "It is important we keep it hidden. As for your doll—you may keep her, but only inside our home. Do you understand?"

"Yes, Papa."

"Whenever you are angry or frightened," he said, "I want you to place your hand over your bracelet and count to three."

Closing my eyes, I wrapped my cold fingers around my new bracelet and counted to three. Although I couldn't see my wings disappear, I felt it.

Smiling lovingly at me, Papa rubbed my cheek and kissed my forehead. As he got up, my mother turned away. Although I couldn't make out what they were saying, I knew it had something to do with my mother being afraid for our lives. She kept arguing, while my father did his best to reassure her that no matter what I *was*, we'd make it work.

I picked up my injured Alice and held her close to my heart. "You are well," I said, brushing her straw hair back.

The second I looked up, my heart nearly stopped.

Right behind our meat-roasting pit was a woman standing in the shadows, the hood of her long green cloak making it almost impossible to see her face. Around her neck was a clear quartz pendant held together by hemp rope. On this rope were little black bits. At first, I thought these to be pieces of dirt or oil stains, but every few seconds, one of them sparkled.

The woman smiled at me—a smile that made me want to run up and hug her.

Then, I noticed her left hand. While there may not have been any blood, there were no fingers, either.

I glanced down at my doll, whose hand matched this woman's.

How was this even possible?

When I looked up again, however, she was gone.

CHAPTER 12

"You're my fucking doll," I blurt.

I don't mean to be so rude about it, but I can't contain my surprise. This whole time, my protection has been some woman following me. What is she? Some illusion? Is she even real? I'm tempted to reach for her wrinkled face, but that would elevate my level of rudeness.

She offers a plain smile—one that says, *There's a lot more to this than you know, but I don't have the time to explain it.*

"You had better hurry, Alexis," she says. "Your time within the Hall of Hallows is limited."

Again with the lack of clear instructions. Why didn't Peter tell me this? If this is what the guy does for a living, he needs to find a new job.

Instead of arguing with her, I shove Alice—the doll, not the real-life version—into my pocket and the old woman disappears instantly.

Clenching my teeth, I close my eyes and throw myself into the flames.

At first, the heat reminds me of my village all

those years ago. It's hot—sizzling hot—but it doesn't seem to hurt. At least not physically. What pains me the most is the memory of watching everything burn to the ground.

Suddenly, I remember seeing Alice all those years ago. As I ran from the fire, she stood at the edge of the forest, the hood of her green cloak masking her face entirely. I remember trying to run toward her, but no matter how fast I ran, I couldn't reach her.

Had she been the one to guide me to safety?

I'm dying to know more about this woman, but first, I have to deal with finding Devania.

The heat surrounding me disappears as fast as it came and I find myself standing in the same forest I walked through earlier.

For real?

Did the fire send me back a step?

While everything might look the same, something's different. I can't quite put my finger on it, but it doesn't feel like I'm standing in the same forest.

"You must be Alexis," comes a woman's voice.

I flinch at the sound of my name and turn around. What's up with people always appearing behind me? Is it so goddamn difficult to appear in *front* of me?

The woman smiles the moment I make eye contact with her.

I don't bother asking her how she knows my

name. It feels like everyone knows my name these days, and not for reasons I'd like them to.

She appears to be my age, maybe a little older. And by my age, I mean the age I appear to be—around the thirty-year-old mark.

I'm afraid to imagine what anyone would look like at a thousand years old. A walking skeleton, maybe. I smile at the thought, but when I realize she's staring me cold in the face, I tighten my lips.

From the top of her head extending down around her shoulders is a long red cloak with a golden strip decorating its edges. The cloak floats over her shoulders as if sitting on two thick pads underneath, giving off a royalty vibe.

What is she, exactly? She isn't pale—at least not *vampire* pale. She's stunning in every sense of the word with golden eyes so fierce they almost look orange, long auburn hair that disappears into her cloak, and full red lips to match. She reminds me of Little Red Riding Hood—someone I hope to never meet. Anyone who isn't a feeble knows *she's* the wolf, and a conniving, dangerous one at that.

I breathe in, trying to catch a hint of her scent.

Pumpkin spice mixed with candle wax. I know that smell. She's a Ukrisse demon, also known as a Morpher. So now the question is, who is she *really*? And is she even a *she*? This demon could be anyone or anything.

"You must be wondering who I am," she says.

No shit, Batman.

"May I ask who you're looking for?" she asks.

There's a calmness to her that makes it impossible for me to stay angry. I'm tired, hungry—in more ways than one—and craving alcohol more than oxygen.

"I'm looking for the Black Widow," I say.

She elevates her chin, almost inquisitively.

Okay, so this lady's interested in what I have to say. Maybe I'm reaching the end of this dumbass trial at last. Why isn't she responding? Is there another secret code I'm supposed to know about?

"I was sent by Veerka," I add.

Her eyes widen slightly, which tells me she knows who Veerka is.

"Your friend is in danger," she says.

"Veerka?" I say, clenching my fists. "What kind of danger?"

"Not Veerka," she says. "The witch."

Rachel? Is that who she's talking about? First of all, we aren't friends. But what's she talking about? What's going on with Rachel? My mouth goes dry and I take a step forward.

"What do you mean, she's in danger?"

"The Zerachu you met isn't who she says she is."

You have got to be kidding me.

Is this some sick kind of joke? Like I already don't have enough on my plate?

I part my lips to make a snarky comment when half her figure flickers as if on the verge of disappearing entirely.

"We're running out of time," she says. "Here, take this."

With her arm straight out, she takes a step forward. I meet her halfway and open my palm. When she loosens her grasp, a silver ring with a finely carved red ruby falls out.

"What's this?" I ask.

"It's a communication device," she says. "It's also how other members of the Battalion will recognize you."

What's she talking about? I slide my thumb across the ring's shiny, squared-off surface and raise it to my eye. It doesn't look like it has any sort of camera or microphone in it. And I would know—that's been my job for years. Have they gotten *that* good at concealing surveillance cameras since I last purchased my equipment?

"It's magic," she says plainly.

Now I feel like an idiot. Of course, it's magic.

"Who's the Battalion?" I ask.

"We are," she says.

And then it hits me.

"You're Devania," I say.

She offers a hint of a smile—a look that says, *You're correct, but don't get too excited yet.*

Half of her silhouette flickers again, and this time, her left arm disappears entirely.

"What do I do with this?" I ask, slipping the Battalion ring onto my middle index finger.

She said something about people of the

Battalion being able to recognize me, so I assume the ring's got some sort of magical properties that allow it to become visible to those wearing a similar ring.

"If you need to speak with me, press your thumb over the ruby and call out my name three times. I will only appear if you truly need me."

It's like I'm in some twisted version of *The Wizard of Oz*. Then again, it shouldn't surprise me. The number three is meaningful in the world of magic.

"Anyone wearing one belongs to the Battalion," she continues. "They are your allies. And whatever you do—don't lose the thing. It possesses magic powerful enough to destroy an entire city."

It's hard to imagine that a rebellion group leader would allow so many people to wear something this powerful. Then again, it's obvious by the whole trial thing that they don't want to let anyone into the group.

I guess I'm not so bad after all.

"These rings were forged from the same metals as the Heart of Danu," she says.

Why does that sound so familiar? The Heart of Danu? Oh, shit. That's the talisman Rachel was looking for—the one I found hidden in plain sight in the garden of one of my marks, Adam Shaw. I spent so many days binge drinking afterward that I almost forgot about it. Rachel wanted that thing, and I'd promised her I'd give it to her if she helped me find Veerka, which she did.

Devania's talking about it like it's one of the most powerful items in the world. For something to be forged of the *same* metal? Like it's sacred, or something.

Is the talisman *that* powerful? Did I fuck up again by handing it over to a kid?

"Yeah, about that—" I say.

She flickers again, and this time, the corner of her lip and chin becomes invisible.

"Hurry, Alexis. Your friend needs you."

"What about Veerka? And Lucius and the rest of the vampires? That's why she sent me here."

I don't mean to come across as desperate, but the chick's about to disappear and there's no telling when I'll get to talk to her again. She said I could touch the ring to call for her, but even then, she made it sound like it's an emergency-only type of thing.

"Everything is connected, Alexis." She turns her partial head sideways as if someone is moving toward her. With wide eyes, she looks at me again. "That's all I can tell you right now. Go! Hurry!"

CHAPTER 13

The next thing I know, I'm standing inside the staff room Peter the Ratiken led me through earlier. This time, however, something's different. Although I know I was standing here before entering the trial, it doesn't quite feel the same.

Goddamn it.

Did Devania somehow send me through to another dimension? A different version of our world? It wouldn't be the first time this happened.

Where's Peter? Where is everyone? My heartbeat quickens, and I rush out of the staff room.

The second I step out into the Red Lounge, my stomach sinks.

Where is everyone? The entire casino is empty. Slot machines are silent, poker tables vacant, and the air around me is colder than usual. It's so quiet I can hear my breath. That and the air coming from the ventilation system.

What the fuck happened? Is this what Devania was talking about? Wasting no time, I run as fast as

I can to the elevator and press the button.

It dings, the sound echoing loudly as if being emitted through a speakerphone.

The ride up feels like it'll never end. I'm freaking out inside. How could everything have changed so much within a few hours?

The second I reach the twenty-sixth floor, I swipe my card through my hotel room's card slot and wait for the signal to turn green.

Nothing happens. Why isn't it opening? I swipe it again. Nothing.

"Hello?" I shout, now blasting my fist against the door.

Something's wrong.

Gripping the handle, I nudge my shoulder into the door and it bursts open.

Thank the goddesses for my super strength.

When I step foot inside my hotel room, I'm not surprised to find it empty. Where is everyone? Something happened. I'm not sure what it is yet, but I intend to find out.

In the lounge area are my empty beer bottles, which means no one has come by to clean up. If that's the case, then whatever happened must have happened soon after I went into the Hall of Hallows, and it must have affected the entire Dark Hall.

Here's what I'd like to know: how long was I *actually* in there?

Did time mess up? That tends to happen when

traveling through dimensions or toying with reality. Did I even leave the Hall of Hollows? Am I still there now?

Time.

That's what I need to find.

Rushing across the room, I make my way over to the hotel room's telephone. It looks more like a display unit than anything with its wide screen, small speaker, and sleek white design.

At the corner of the screen is a time and date stamp:

3:03 a.m., April 17

What the fuck? It was the eleventh yesterday. This thing has got to be busted. No way has that much time passed without Rachel trying to find me through one of her portals.

I'm tempted to rub my Battalion ring, but I have a hunch Devania won't be in the mood to see me so soon. Besides, for all I know, this is another test.

I'm about to head over to the fridge to ease my soul with a nice cold beer when a small slip of paper catches my eye. It looks like a tattered sticky note left for a month in someone's back pocket.

The writing is poor—childlike, even.

Couldn't find u anywhere. Zerachu weird. Stole the rest of my book and talisman. Drax and I had to evacuate with everyone.

PS: Took ur wallet 4 money 4 motel. Lucky Cheetah. 308.

Rachel.

Shit. Is she trying to tell me that she's lost the entire *Book of Origin* now? First, the vampires sent by Lucius stole some of its pages, and now she's lost the rest. And on top of that, the Heart of Danu was taken, too. This is why I didn't want a young fucking witch holding on to something so powerful.

What was I thinking?

Closing my eyes, I inhale the seductive smell of beer while gliding its cool glass lip across mine. I want this more than anything, but I also know that shit just got real. It takes everything in me to put the bottle down, but I do it.

This is the first time I ever hear of the Dark Hall being evacuated, which means things are bad.

Beyond bad.

Now, some evil and powerful witch has the *Book of Origin* and the Heart of Danu.

We're all fucked.

CHAPTER 14

The Lucky Cheetah looks like someone built it for the sole purpose of allowing underpaid prostitutes to do their jobs. It's surely owned by a slumlord or a pimp. Everything about it screams dirty, rundown, and cheap. Even the sign hangs on an angle, and from where I'm standing, it looks like a pair of panties are stuck on the giant L.

I go to room number 308 like Rachel's note instructed and knock on the door. I know I'm at the right place when Mr. Mushroom barks and claws at the front door.

Sometimes, I think he wishes he were a Rottweiler. Either that or he *thinks* he is.

Several door locks unlatch and Rachel's face appears in a narrow crack between the doorframe and the door, a rusted chain dangling across her forehead.

I suck on my front teeth and grab my hips as if to say, *Well, you gonna let me in, or what?*

Quickly, she unlatches the chain and flings the door open.

Barging in, I say, "You steal my wallet and you get a room in a shithole like this?"

"I was trying to save you money," Rachel says.

I should be thanking her, but I'm filthy rich now. The last thing I want to do is hang out in a place that reminds me of my apartment.

At the other end of the room, Drax sits on the one bed in the room with smoke floating around his head. When he catches me watching him, he slaps the air in front of him and coughs. "It's about time."

"About time?" I say. "What the fuck is going on?"

Drax and Rachel exchange a look, which leads me to believe I'm missing something.

"We should be asking you that," Drax says. "You ditched us for a week and then shit hit the fan at the casino. Where the hell have you been?"

My jaw hangs loose. A week? How is that even possible?

"What're you talking about, Drax? I was gone for a few hours."

With bloodshot eyes, Drax stares at me the way he does when he's trying to figure out if I'm drunk, high, or both.

"It's been a week, Alex."

Tucking my thumb inside my jeans, I pull at them.

"Oh, shit," I say. "That's why these things feel loose on me. I haven't eaten in a week."

"Where were you?" Drax asks.

Shaking my head, I move toward the fridge. The

moment I open it, Red bubbles inside of me, begging to be released. Why is it empty? Drax knows better than to not have alcohol available for me.

"You need a clear head," he says before I can turn around and glare at him.

I squeeze the fridge's handle so hard it snaps off and Rachel lets out a gasp.

"I will be clear," I say through clenched teeth, "once I get something in me."

Rachel points at a pile of junk food next to Drax. "We got chips."

Mr. Mushroom barks, jumps on the bed, and shoves his head in one of the half-eaten bags. Riskus grabs one of the unopened bags, opens his mouth nearly as wide as his body, and eats the whole thing in one gulp.

"Hey!" I shout.

Riskus freezes with a bag of chips hanging out of his mouth and Mr. Mushroom flattens his ears and cowers next to Drax.

"What the hell are you doing feeding my dog this shit?" I snap.

Rachel shrugs. "I got him kibble," she says, pointing at an ugly folded bag that looks like it's been sitting in storage for years. "But he won't eat it."

"No shit," I say. "I only feed him premium."

"It says premium on the bag," Rachel says.

"Rachel, half the writing on that bag is in

Chinese. I've never even heard of the brand. It's probably full of cat meat or some shit."

"Whoa," Rachel says. "What are you, a racist?"

"Racist?" I sneer. "Cut the sensitivity bullshit, kid. Just because it's a stereotype doesn't mean it isn't true or that I mean it as an insult. Do your research and you'll see that cat meat is a thing in some parts of China."

She turns to Drax, but he knows better than to get involved in an argument with me.

"I'm heading out for a drink. When I get back, I expect answers."

"All right, all right," Drax says, sticking an arm up in the air. "There's vodka under the bed."

I glower at him until I feel like my eyes are about to seal themselves shut. "Why are you only telling me this now?"

"Why do you think, Alex? A lot is going on, and all you want to do is get drunk. When are you going to get over what happened? This isn't healthy. You're diminishing yourself and putting everyone's lives at risk by fucking with your powers." The muscles in his jaw pop out and his eyes go red. I've seen Drax's eyes go red twice—both of which occurred during a life-or-death situation. With his incisor teeth bared at me, he lets out a hissing breath. "I was hoping that maybe for once, you'd realize how serious things were and you'd agree to be sober for a bit."

Drax's right about everything, but I don't want

to hear it. Especially not right now.

Scoffing, I reach under the bed and pull out the new bottle of Grey Goose. "At least you didn't go cheap on this."

The redness in his eyes shimmers as I crack the bottle open and bring it to my lips. But it isn't his eyes that cause me to hesitate—it's Rachel's. From my peripheral, I can sense her watching me the way she might have her father when he threw fits of rage.

It makes me feel like a complete fuckup.

Sighing, I twist the cap back on and toss the bottle on the bed beside Drax. His face lights up, almost as if he's witnessed some miraculous event. I may not be a mind reader, but the confused look on his face translates to, *Did I seriously talk you out of drinking for the first time in months?*

Ignoring him, I dig my fingernails into my palms. "Okay. Spill. What the fuck happened over there? Is this about Zerachu being someone else?"

I'm surprised I remember what Devania told me, seeing as I almost never care enough about other people's problems to retain information. In any other situation, I may not have given a shit, but Devania specifically told me that Rachel was in danger.

While I might not want to give a shit about the kid, she's now my responsibility and after everything I put her through, I owe her my protection at the very least.

Rachel pulls out a wooden chair tucked underneath a cheap computer desk and sits down. Leaning the weight of her body on an armrest, she focuses her attention on the carpet, her red brows almost touching over the bridge of her nose.

"Something's wrong with her, Alexis," she says. "I thought the Great Witch was supposed to be some powerful witch who protects people."

"She is," I say.

"Well, she didn't protect anyone. She ripped the book right out of my hands and the talisman off my neck."

Zerachu would never do that. The woman has spent centuries working toward maintaining peace in the Underworld. She may be cold and unapologetic at times, but she isn't evil.

"She wouldn't do that," I say.

Rachel offers me a shrug. "Maybe she was cursed or something."

It's almost impossible to believe that Zerachu might be cursed. She's one of the most—if not *the* most—powerful witches alive. She might offer fortune-telling for fun, but everyone knows that witch controls the Dark Hall. None of this makes any sense.

Sighing, I sit at the edge of the bed and Mr. Mushroom lunges at me like he hasn't seen me in months. The second I look at him, his ears go flat and he curls into a ball against my thigh.

"It's okay, buddy," I say, scratching his forehead.

In reality, that statement couldn't be further from the truth.

Nothing is okay.

The *Book of Origin*—the most powerful book known to shadow dwellers—along with the Heart of Danu—another dangerous item seemingly used to amplify magical abilities—is now in the wrong hands.

In short: we're all fucked.

Chapter 15

"Is she okay?" Rachel says in the distance.

Drax responds, but I'm too busy staring at the wall to understand.

There has to be an answer.

"She's been sitting there for hours," Rachel says.

Zerachu wouldn't do anything to put the Underworld at risk, which leads me to believe either one of two things:

1) She was under some sort of spell.

2) It wasn't her.

Are either of those options even possible? It's hard to imagine anyone casting a spell over her. That woman would smell an attempt miles away and turn her attacker into fungi.

Which leads me to option two.

But could someone else have impersonated her? I saw her a few hours before Rachel did; she looked fine to me. This isn't adding up.

"She isn't even blinking," Rachel says.

"She's thinking," Drax responds.

Riskus goes on to say something, but it sounds

like nothing more than high-pitched gibberish.

"Would you guys shut up?" I hiss, and the motel room goes quiet. "I'm trying to think."

"You've been thinking for hours," Rachel says. "How much longer will this take?"

Finally, I turn my head toward everyone. "As long as it takes."

"Well, I'm hungry," Rachel says.

Rolling my eyes, I reach into my pocket, whip out my wallet, and toss it at her. "Then go get some food."

It bounces a few times off her palms until she finally catches it.

"You guys staying here?" she asks.

Rather than answer her, I go back to staring at the wall. As I disappear into my thoughts, Rachel marches across the motel room with Riskus prancing behind her. The moment she opens the motel's door, however, a loud bang echoes all around us.

How the fuck am I supposed to concentrate with everyone making so much noise? Gritting my teeth, I scowl up at Rachel, but the horrified look on her face is enough to get me to keep my anger in check.

With her back pressed against the closed door, her chest heaves as she struggles to catch her breath. Her eyes, easily the size of golf balls, dart between me and Drax as if one of us holds the key to calming her down.

"Holy mother of Hades," Drax says, getting up for the first time.

Cautiously, he moves toward the motel's grimy window, pulls one of the blind slats down with his claws, and sticks his face against the glass.

Another explosive sound goes off, and the walls around us tremble. Mr. Mushroom lunges off the bed and disappears underneath.

"What the fuck's going on?" I say, jolting upright.

Shoving Drax aside, I pull at the blinds, tearing them off the wall completely. I didn't mean to pull *that* hard, but what's done is done.

I squint through the window at what appears to be a group of young warlocks swinging wands around. My attention shifts onto the shortest one whose mouth is wide open. He's shouting something, though I can't make out what.

Then, he jabs his wand at a red pickup truck parked in the motel's lot. At once, a stream of green light spits out of the tip of his wand and envelopes the truck, causing its windows to shatter and its tires to explode.

Are you fucking kidding me? Out in broad daylight? They're acting like the Code of Invisibility doesn't apply to them. All shadow dwellers are bound by this law. Morons like these are the type who risk pissing off Asmodeus.

And everyone knows what happens when Asmodeus gets pissed off. Vampires start talking about hunting down and eliminating certain races of fae. They've done it in the past—leading to the extinction of certain demons—and they've made it clear they aren't afraid to do it again.

"Stuff like this has been happening all week," Rachel says. "Ever since we were told to evacuate the Dark Hall, people keep talking about the End of the Divide, or something."

My stomach sinks. This can't be happening. Shadow dwellers have spoken about the End of the Divide for centuries, but the idea has always been that—an idea.

Drax knows what I'm thinking. With a single glance his way, it's like we're reading each other's minds.

"People say shit to say shit," he says, almost as if trying to convince himself.

"I get that, Drax, but this is the first time the Dark Hall gets evacuated," I say.

He remains silent. He knows I'm right. Shadow dwellers are accustomed to running into a few rogues now and then—people who think they can run around casting spells on others, or tearing feebles apart with no fear of consequences.

These shadow dwellers always get caught by the vampires, and no one ever hears about them again.

The End of the Divide isn't a term that's thrown around lightly. It originated centuries ago when groups of shadow dwellers banded together, hoping to unite our world as one. But how can shadow dwellers and feebles coexist? People have tried and failed.

The End of the Divide, if it ever occurs, won't be an amicable union—it'll be a bloodbath. Feebles will stand up and demand that we be confined behind prison bars to protect their families.

Clenching my fists, I stare at the warlocks outside who are now firing strings of light at overhead birds and turning them into honeybees. This is the kind of behavior that will attract feeble aggression.

"I'll be back," I say.

"What're you gonna do, Alex?" Drax says. "Knock them out?" His flared nostrils look like they're on the verge of splitting his face in half. He's as pissed as I am, but I think his anger is coming from a place of hopelessness. "This is bigger than us. I don't see what you, me, or anyone can do about it. You have to let the Council of Elders deal with it."

I scoff. "The Council of Elders?" I don't mean to talk about them like they're less useful than gum stuck to concrete on a hot summer day, but everyone knows that the council got outnumbered centuries ago. Sure, they might still try to uphold the laws of the Underworld, but when all is said and done, the vampires are the ones *truly* in charge.

Personally, this has never made sense to me. Why let the undead rule the world when you have people who have magical abilities? I guess that's politics for you.

"So, what?" I say. "We're supposed to sit in here and wait for some big hero to save the day? The *Book of Origin* was stolen, Drax. I doubt the Elders give a shit about anything other than retrieving it."

"Is that why Zerachu took it?" Rachel asks. "Is she a part of the council?"

Biting my lip, I stare at her. "No, she isn't. And I'm telling you, something's up. Zerachu wouldn't steal it. If anything, she'd want to protect it."

"Maybe that's why she took it," Drax says.

"Yeah," I say, losing my patience. "And what happened after she took it? Things got bad. You think that would have happened if she were only trying to protect it? Why was everyone asked to evacuate?"

Rachel glances at Drax but remains silent, so I pop my eyebrows. "Well?"

"She started shouting a bunch of stuff," Rachel says. "There were lights everywhere and machines exploding."

"Exactly," I say as if Rachel's explanation should be enough to shut everyone up. "Now, you can all sit here like a bunch of wusses, or you can help me get control of the situation outside."

After a moment of silence, Riskus punches his chest and raises his chin like a trained soldier. Rachel, obviously unable to let her minion go out there alone, rolls her eyes and picks up her wand. At my ankles, Mr. Mushroom barks and Drax says, "Fine... Sheesh. I'll come too."

"Good," I say, swinging the door wide open.

I'm about to step out and show these punks what I'm made of when a deafening growl fills the sky above our heads. We all look up, Mr. Mushroom included, his thick tongue hanging out the side of his mouth.

"Holy shit," Rachel breathes.

Overhead, a huge purple-scaled dragon comes soaring through the clouds, its massive leather wings sending a powerful gust of wind into the parking lot. The group of warlocks run away as car alarms go off, bumpers detach, and garbage cans roll across the asphalt. The dragon flies in circles as if searching for something, and every few seconds, lets out a deep roar that makes the hairs on my neck stand up.

It's jaw, which is easily the size of an entire pickup truck, snaps open as hot red flames come blasting down toward a chained bicycle and an old wooden bench, both of which crumble into a pile of ash.

"Fuck that," I say, pushing everyone back inside. "Let's wait for the Council of Elders."

CHAPTER 16

Drax peeks through the window, his neck craned as he searches the clouds. "I don't see it anymore."

"Yeah, well, doesn't mean it's gone," I say. "Unless you're in the mood to be incinerated, I suggest you get away from that window and sit down."

Drax takes a step back, sighs, and reaches across the bed to grab the nearest bag of chips. "We should have gotten more food."

I'm about to grab myself a bag when my ring's reflection catches my eye.

Devania made it clear that she wouldn't appear unless the situation were critical. The thought of calling for her leaves my mind as quickly as it entered. Although this feels critical, I know it isn't. At least not in the grand scheme of things. But it isn't the idea of reaching out to her that has me thinking—it's the ring itself.

"Hey," I say, still staring at my ring. When I realize no one knows who I'm talking to, I point my nose at Rachel. "How good are you at your portals?"

She shrugs. "I mean, I've gotten better. Why do you ask?"

"If I gave you something," I say, "could you create a portal that leads me to its source?"

With her jaw hanging loose and her eyelids flat, she projects pure teenage attitude. Obviously, I'm not making any sense, so I slip off my ring and hold it in front of her face.

"Someone gave this to me. She told me it's made from the same metal as the Heart of Danu."

With a sly smirk, she tilts her head back. "I get it. You want me to try to get you to wherever the stolen talisman is."

"Exactly," I say. "Whoever has it is causing a lot of shit to go down. All I want is to be taken to wherever it is so I can steal it back."

"I imagine that means you want me to leave the portal open," she says.

I give her a sarcastic twitch of the lip meant to signify, *No shit, smart-ass.*

"You do realize that puts us in danger," Rachel says. "And you also realize there's no guarantee this will work. For all I know, I might end up sending you to some faraway mountain where the previous stone came from."

Pinching the bridge of my nose, I close my eyes. "What option do we have, Rachel?" I throw an arm upward, pointing at the dragon through the roof. "Getting burned alive by a dragon or trying to take action? The sooner we get this problem resolved, the sooner that dragon will disappear."

"Maybe the dragon's gone," she points out.

"This isn't about the dragon," I say. "Shit will keep getting worse. Do you understand? This is bad, Rachel. Super bad. I suspect that Zerachu—or whoever was controlling her—is on the hunt for the rest of the book, if they haven't already gotten to it. Don't you get it? A war is starting."

"All because of my grandma's book?"

Admittedly, I feel kind of bad for the kid. She must think all of this is her fault, when it's mine.

A few hours ago, all I could think about was fucking Veerka.

Now, the entire world is about to crumble all because of my selfishness.

I should have been more careful.

I should have been better.

If Jamal were here, he'd be ashamed of me

As my throat swells, I shake my head. "Fuck the past, okay?" I tell her. "This isn't your fault, and it isn't the book's fault. Shit happened, and now we have to deal with it. I'll do whatever I can to get your stuff back, okay? Or at least out of the dangerous hands it landed in." When she doesn't respond, I add, "Can you create the portal, or not?"

Rachel moves toward my ring and sticks out an open palm. Puffing out my cheeks, I tug the ring off.

"Don't lose that," I say, giving her my *I'm the boss* look.

She turns around as if she didn't hear a thing I

said—likely running all sorts of recited spells in her head—and brings the ring up to eye-level.

"So, it's made from the same metal?" she asks.

I nod.

"Okay, I think I can do this."

When I don't respond, she turns to me and says, "Can you guys give me some space, please?"

Mr. Mushroom runs away as if he understands, which I know he does. He's a smart cookie, and I don't give a shit what anyone else says—he understands English. Sometimes I think he's a reincarnated witch. Either that, or he used to be human and someone morphed him into a dog out of spite.

Drax and I move to the back of the motel room and near the bathroom where the stench of mold escapes. It's so strong that I turn to Drax to breathe in his scent of mud, apples, Taiwanese plastic, and weed. I'm thankful he isn't one of those demons who reek of something rotten.

"Riskus," Rachel says, and without questioning her, Riskus reaches into his pocket and pulls out a brown pouch that I assume contains powder.

This isn't the first time I see Riskus give her powder, and now I'm wondering if he has an endless supply of it. Is he wearing some sort of powder-producing pants? I suppose anything is possible these days. Either that or his body creates it. Staring at his long gray hair fastened into a bun, I cringe. Maybe this magical powder she keeps using is nothing more than his dandruff.

She reaches for the pouch, opens it up by its rope strings, and sniffs the contents. "Not that one."

Riskus nods, his fleshy pointed ears wiggling, and reaches for another pouch. When he hands it to her, she opens it and pours a few grains into her palm. The stuff is orange and clunky, reminding me of pink Himalayan salt.

"That'll work," she says, squeezing her fist around the pouch.

Riskus grins from ear to ear, making him look like a smiling great white shark. It's obvious he wants praise, so she pats him on the head and adds, "Good job."

Rachel pours a teaspoon worth of the salt-looking grains into her palm, closes her eyes, and recites a bunch of gibberish. Considering she started creating portals recently, I have to hand it to her—the kid's a genius. I've seen her cast some spells after reading them a single time in her spell books. It's almost like she's able to retain every single piece of information that enters her brain.

Maybe her grandmother *was* something special.

As I watch her sprinkle the orange dust into the air, I wonder if maybe Rachel possesses the same capabilities as Zerachu. They are related, after all. Maybe I don't give her enough credit. Someone once told me that witches who are fortunate enough to attend witching school often require years of experience before being able to create a portal. And even then, most schools refuse to include this in their curriculums due to the dangers of traveling through time and space.

But Rachel? The kid hasn't even gone to witching school and she's already creating them.

Mr. Mushroom whimpers and licks his nose when a frizzy orange light swirls around the room. It forms an oval shape, twirling in circles the way storm clouds do before sending a devastating tornado to the ground.

The brighter the color gets, the faster the portal spins. Rachel flicks her wand left and right, and her long red hair flows behind her as if she were standing in front of a giant fan.

It gets so intense that I'm forced to pull my hair out of my face.

"It's ready!" she shouts over the loud humming.

I glance sideways at Drax as if to say, *Wish me luck*, and he returns a look with slanted hairless brows that doesn't reassure me whatsoever.

Moving toward the portal, I shout, "Close it in five minutes."

"What if you aren't back?" Rachel says.

I don't answer her, which is an answer in itself. It shouldn't take me more than five minutes to grab that talisman and jump back into the portal. If it does, it means something happened and I can't risk anyone else coming back into this room if I'm not here.

Rachel might be developing as a witch, but she and Drax are no match against evil beings.

I pull my long black hair back into a high ponytail and tie it with the elastic I always keep around my wrist. Sucking in a deep breath, I turn to Rachel, who stands awkwardly as if debating whether to hug me before I leave. But before giving her the chance to get all mushy, I say, "I'll be back," and I step into the portal.

CHAPTER 17

I breathe in, feeling intoxicated.

That smell.

I know that smell.

Where am I?

I blink once, then twice to figure out what's going on. Did I even leave our room? Everything around me looks the same, but Mr. Mushroom, Drax, Rachel, and Riskus are nowhere to be seen.

Did she send me into another dimension?

"What the fuck?" I say aloud.

"You," comes a familiar voice.

Snapping my wrist blades out, I swing around, prepared to go for the kill.

But the second I lay eyes on him, I stiffen.

"You," I say right back.

I should be interrogating him, but how can I? He steps out of the motel's bathroom wearing nothing but a towel wrapped around his waist, his muscular abs popping out above the fold. He runs a hand through his freshly washed hair, his bicep bulging, and then over his short and scruffy beard—which, might I add, looks fucking sexy on him.

I part my lips to say something, but nothing comes out.

What the hell is wrong with me?

He smirks like he knows what I'm thinking. I know that look; I give it to feebles all the time. Now I know what the problem is... and it isn't *me*.

"Would you stop it?" I say.

"Stop what?" he says nonchalantly.

"Stop trying to seduce me!"

I know he's doing it because he used his powers on me in Adam Shaw's house. I didn't know it at the time, but this guy's an incubus, which means he has the same powers as me. We came close to screwing but some asshole witch who tried to turn me into a pile of ashes rudely interrupted us.

He cocks a brow. "I have to protect myself."

I scowl at him. "Protect yourself from what?"

"Isn't it obvious?" he says. "From you."

I let out a laugh—something that feels foreign to me. "I get it. You're trying to seduce me to avoid me seducing you."

His lip pulls up on one side, revealing a few bleach-white teeth. "Precisely."

"Well," I say, my eyes making their way to his towel. "You can stop. I promise I won't use my powers on you."

He doesn't seem convinced, but I'm not backing down. Then, his attention shifts to the portal behind me.

"What're you doing here?" he says.

"Getting my friend's talisman back," I say. "Now hand it over."

He stares at me like I've lost my mind. "What're you talking about?"

"Don't play stupid, asshole," I say. "This portal sent me to—" but I stop myself short when something shiny catches my eye. I point at his hand and the silver ring with a red ruby around his index finger. "A Battalion ring," I breathe. "Where'd you get that?"

With his other hand, he covers it as if trying to protect it from me while his gaze shifts to my ringless hand. "How do you know what this is?"

"I have the same thing," I say, flicking my ringless hand in the air. "Well, my witch friend has it. That's how I got here."

"I'm not following," he says. "What do you want with the talisman?"

"I'm trying to get it back," I say.

His stare narrows. "So am I."

I want to believe that this guy's sincere—I mean, he has a Battalion ring. Devania made it clear that anyone who wears one is an ally.

"So, we're on the same team," I say, cautiously.

"It would appear so," he says.

An awkward moment of silence fills the room until finally, the portal behind me disappears with a loud swoosh.

"There goes my ride," I say. "Where am I?"

Rubbing his chin, he gives me a full up-and-down. It's a look that tells me he's trying to figure out whether I'm confused or downright crazy. I take the opportunity to stare at his smooth chest and chiseled abs.

"Let me get this straight," he says, rubbing his scruff. "You jumped into a portal without knowing where you were going?"

"I knew where—would you put a fucking shirt on?" I snap.

Shaking his head, he lets out an amused laugh and reaches for a plain white T-shirt sitting at the edge of the motel bed. He slips it on, almost too slowly, as if wanting me to take it all in before it's gone.

He glides his hands over his T-shirt to flatten the creases, raises his chin, and crosses his arms. "You're in motel room 309 and I'm beginning to think you're following me."

"Motel room 309? Are you fucking—"

With clenched fists, I storm toward the front door.

"I wouldn't do that if I were you," comes his deep, soothing voice.

With my fingers wrapped around the door handle's shitty metal, I turn around. "Wouldn't do what? Leave? Am I your prisoner now?"

He's still smiling, and it creates the strangest sensation in me. I want to have my way with him and punch him in the face all at once. I'm not used to men, or women, being so cocky around me. It's usually the other way around.

"There's a dragon out there."

I pinch my eyebrow to hold in my anger. "It's still out there?"

"Yes, it is."

"That's fine," I say. "I don't need the door."

Without hesitating, I march straight toward the side of the motel room where a cheesy painting of a half-naked woman hangs crookedly. With a tight fist, I punch a hole through her face and the drywall.

A beam of wood splits and bits of drywall fall to the ground. Extracting my claws, I grab whatever I can and tear back. The painting splits in half and flies behind me, missing the incubus's face by an inch. In front of me is a now huge, gaping hole in the wall.

Through it, Rachel stands with eyes so big you'd think she was having an allergic reaction.

Sticking my face in the hole, I say, "I asked you to send me to the talisman, kid. Your spell didn't work. All it did was send me to the nearest item made of the same metal."

She opens her mouth and it makes a sticky sound, but nothing comes out.

Chapter 18

I'm not sure what's more frustrating—the fact that Rachel's portal didn't work as planned, or the fact that it led me to the one person I now can't stop fantasizing about. As I pace back and forth in his room, he watches me. Behind me, Rachel does the same thing with her face pressed up against the hole.

"Are you going to say something?" he asks.

I stop walking and shift my weight onto one leg. "Sure. For starters, what the hell's your name?"

He seems amused by my attitude. I'm bitchy because I'm getting hungry. Who the hell am I supposed to feed off of? As much as I want to pin this guy down on the bed, how can I trust him? He's an incubus. If things get out of control, there's a good chance he'll suck me dry.

I like to believe that I'm stronger than that... that *he's* the one who should be afraid, but he's powerful, and with the amount of alcohol I've had coursing through my bloodstream over the last few years, I suspect I'm at a disadvantage.

I mean, come on. Teleportation? Seriously? I haven't let that one go. The guy clicked his fingers when we were in Adam's basement and disappeared instantly.

I'm beyond jealous.

I must be glaring hard at him. He reaches for his face, glances over at Rachel, and says, "What? Do I have something on my face?"

Seems he's a comedian, too.

How much more perfect can this guy get?

Clearing my throat, I roll my eyes. "You gonna tell me your name, or not?"

"Ace. Ace Hendrix. And you are?"

Ace and Alexis... now that's hot.

"Sorry?" I say, realizing I disappeared into my head again.

He raises his nose in the air and sizes me up. "Your name."

"Alexis," I say like he's wasting my time. "Alexis Rayne."

The short grains of his beard follow the rising of his cheeks as he grins. "Alexis. It suits you."

I make a conscious effort not to cross my arms. "Why's that?"

"It means helper or defender."

I scoff. "Right. That suits me."

I suspect this guy isn't buying into my whole *fuck off and leave me alone* vibe.

"You came here looking for the Heart of Danu, didn't you?" he says.

I don't respond. How can I? I know where he's going with this and I'd be an idiot to argue with him. He's right—I'm trying to do the right thing, even though I'll never admit it to him, to myself, or anyone, for that matter.

The air around us gets heavy and quiet until finally, Ace clears his throat—a deep rumble that makes me want to tear off his shirt and run my hands across those bulging muscles of his.

For fuck's sake.

"I think we need to create a plan," Ace says.

He's got organizational skills, too. He can organize me any day.

For fuck's sake, Alexis. Shut up.

"I think that's a good idea," comes Rachel's voice.

Drax's face suddenly appears through the hole. "What's a good idea? What's going on here?"

Without responding, I bend down, pick up the painting of the naked woman I punched a hole through, and hang it in front of Drax's face.

He disappears almost entirely, leaving his yellow eye to peep through the woman's torn vagina.

"Hey!" he says.

He blinks between her thighs.

It's a bit freaky to look at, so I say, "Would you get away from the wall? This doesn't concern you. You guys are distracting me."

The truth is, Ace is the one distracting me, but

he's about all the distraction I can handle.

Without saying a word, Drax backs away and covers the hole with a towel.

The moment he disappears, I sense Ace's gaze lingering on me.

"Are you planning to have your way with me?" he asks.

My knees buckle and I catch myself against the crooked painting.

Son of a bitch.

I force a laugh—it's choppy, loud, and awkward, but it eases the tension. I'm not used to anyone being dominant with me—not like this.

"I have no intention of fucking you," I lie.

God... All I want to do is have my way with you.

As much as I want him, I need to be the one who decides when and where it happens. If I give him that power, I'm done for.

He smirks at me, a playful charm about him, and it's obvious he's aware of the power struggle going on in my head. The question is... Who'll break first?

"Oh, I beg to differ, Miss Rayne."

"Alexis," I correct.

He locks his fingers together, his golden eyes making him look like a wild animal. "While I find your first name rather pleasant, you aren't quite ready to own it."

I laugh out loud again—so loud this time that the painting next to my face shifts positions. "What the hell's that supposed to mean? It's my name."

"Since when?"

He knows how this works, which leads me to wonder: how many identity changes has he gone through? How old is this guy?

"What does it matter?" I say.

He shrugs nonchalantly, making me want to grab him by the collar and shake him. "I suppose it doesn't. It's quite a shame you aren't living up to your full potential."

Is this guy insulting me? I part my lips to give him a piece of my mind when he raises his open hands to his perfectly chiseled jaw. "I mean no offense, Miss Rayne. I can see a fire in you, yet I can also see that something is choking it."

Choking me? Mmm. You can choke me anytime, big boy...

"What are you, a therapist?" I hiss. "'Cause I already have one, thanks."

Although I'm fuming inside, I'm also vulnerable and confused. For the first time in centuries, it seems like someone sees *me*. It's an awful feeling— as if he can see all my weaknesses and has zero issues exposing them for what they are.

Clearing his throat, he reaches for a bottle of gel, squirts it into his palm, and rubs it through his wet hair. The cool, crisp scent fills the room and I breathe in a bit longer than necessary. "I should get changed," he says.

With that, he releases his towel and it falls to his ankles.

The moment my eyes roll toward the precise area I'm trying not to think about, I suck in too much air and cough out what feels like an entire lung.

"Are you okay?" he says smoothly, staring at me as if being half-naked is normal.

I avoid glancing his way again and instead turn toward the window. "I'm fine. Hurry up and get dressed."

Although I can't see him, I can *feel* his enticing smile directed at me, and I can see him clearly in my mind now... *All* of him.

He's throwing you off your game, Alexis.

Maybe it's time I do the same to him.

CHAPTER 19

Crossing his arms, Ace stares at me until I cave.

"Fine! But I swear to Hera, if you get me mixed up with some fly and fuck up this perfect physique—"

"It doesn't work that way," he assures me. "I'm not some teleportation machine. The magic won't jumble you up into millions of pieces and reconstruct you. My magic allows you to travel through a dimensional portal."

It still doesn't make sense to me, but the only way out of this place without getting scorched by the dragon is to disappear, and as it turns out, Ace can project his teleportation abilities onto other people.

"So, all we have to do is touch?" I ask.

"Exactly."

He's calm, collected, and effortless when he speaks. Is this why I can't stop thinking about him? He's the polar opposite of me, and it's almost as if our energies are meant to fuse like two puzzle pieces. Mine's chaotic and overbearing, and here he is, acting as if everything is going to be fine even though two of the most powerful items on Earth have ended up in the wrong hands.

He smiles down at me, his plush lips rising higher on one side, and it takes all my willpower not to kiss him.

"Are you using your Lure on me?" I ask.

"My what?"

Lure is the term I use for my seduction. I suppose it makes sense that he'd have his own terminology.

"Are you using magic to seduce me?" I say. "I told you to stop."

"I obeyed," he says.

I elevate my chin. "Do you like to obey?"

Excitement flashes in his eyes. "I suppose it depends on who's giving the command."

What the fuck is he doing? It's like he's toying with me.

Without another word, he moves toward the bed, bends down, and pulls up what appears to be a weapons chest.

"What's that?" I ask.

With a naughty smile that translates to, *You'll see*, he lifts the cover and reaches inside.

But I'm too curious to stand around and wait, so I march toward him and peek into the box.

Stakes, blades, katanas, nunchucks, crossbows, and even pistols.

I'm immediately reminded of the crossbow I

stole from Jamieson and wish I'd taken it along with me. Something like that would be useful right about now.

"I see you're prepared," I say.

"Always."

As I lean forward, inspecting everything his weapon's box has to offer, I breathe him in. I can't get over how delicious this man smells. Demons aren't known for their pleasant fragrances. Then again, I've been told I smell like roses, spearmint, and ecstasy, whatever that means. It must have something to do with being a succubus. Our livelihoods depend on our ability to seduce people.

Although I don't look at him, I can sense him observing me.

"Do you have any idea how dangerous you would be if you allowed yourself to bloom toward your full potential?" he asks.

Slowly, I turn, our faces inches away from one another. His lips, plush and carmine red, are silently yelling at me to touch them with mine. What I wouldn't do to scrape my nails through that sexy stubble of his.

"Why is this happening?" I breathe as if under a hypnotic spell.

He smiles. "Because you're weak."

Taken aback by his words, I'm shaken out of my trance. "Excuse me?"

"Like I already told you, *Rayne*, I mean no disrespect."

"My name's Alexis, and so we're clear, you *are* being disrespectful."

He smirks, clearly amused by my aggravation. "Your name might be Alexis, but it doesn't suit you. At least, not yet."

This guy is getting on my last nerve. What's up with his code language? It's like everything he says has some big secret meaning behind it.

Clenching my fist, I raise it by my face, prepared to bash in that sexy mug of his. "I'm anything but weak."

He doesn't flinch or pull away. His eyes roll from my fist to my eyes, to my lips, and then my body.

Is he checking me out? Or is he sizing me up? What the fuck is going on?

Still smiling, he snatches my wrist and I'm unable to pull away.

What the fuck? How is he so strong? He doesn't hurt me, and it's apparent that he doesn't want to. Instead, he's trying to prove a point.

"Go on," he says. "Pull away."

Fuming, I breathe out hard through my nose and tug back. "I can't."

In any other situation, his strong grip would make me want to tell him to take me until the sun goes down. But this isn't any other situation. I'm weak and vulnerable—both of which I despise more than anything.

If I were human, I'd likely attribute my lack of strength to the fact that my opponent is male.

Biologically, men are bigger and stronger. Of course, there are always exceptions. But I'm not a woman, and Ace is no man. We're both demons, and when it comes to demon strength, muscle size has no bearing on one's strength.

Is he *that* much more powerful than me?

I'm not used to this, and if anything, it's causing Red to want to come out.

My face must be swelling in anger. Gently, he lets me go and redirects his attention to his weapons box as if nothing happened.

"What're you trying to prove?" I lash out.

Nonchalantly, he fastens two metallic plates around his wrists and snaps on a holster belt. "I want you to open your eyes, Rayne."

"Would you stop talking in code and fucking spit it out already?"

He turns toward me again, this time, his eyes searching me. "You have no idea, do you?"

Full-blown attitude spreads across my face. If I open my mouth, I won't be nice, so instead, I wait for him to talk.

"Do you know who your real birth parents are?"

How does my childhood have anything to do with what's going on here? More importantly, how could he know that my parents abandoned me? He must see that I'm freaking out inside. Shaking his head, he reaches into the box again and extracts a slick black crossbow.

"It isn't my place to explain your history to you."

"Then whose is it?" I ask.

I'm not the kind of woman who likes to tiptoe around a subject. If something needs to be said, it should be said exactly how it's meant. I hate reading between the lines or being told I'll understand something at a later time. Why can't I understand it *now*?

"Fucking spit it out."

"I can sense you're irritated," he says.

"You think?"

I'm about to reconsider smashing my fist into his face when the roof over our heads cracks, splits in half, and crumbles to ashes. I cough, wave my hand in front of my face, and cough some more.

An explosive roar rains from the sky, and I reach for my ears.

Standing on the roof of Rachel and Drax's room is the dragon we saw flying earlier. With its mouth agape, it blows out another fiery blast, sending hot flames straight toward Ace and me.

It's one of those oh-shit moments in which you realize you don't have the time to do anything. In a split second, Ace throws himself on top of me, his massive dragon-like wings forming a dome-shaped shield around us. We land next to the bed, the weight of his body holding me down.

Wincing, he breathes out, his warm breath making it even hotter in here. "Fuck!"

With wide eyes, I stare up at him from within the darkness. "You okay?"

He's in too much pain to answer, likely due to his wings being scorched.

"I can't fly like this," he says urgently. He swallows hard, an audible gulp. "I'd teleport us out of here, but I might not have the strength to come back for your friends. You ready to fight?"

"What's your plan?" I ask.

"I'll distract it. You find a way to cut off its—"

"You're wasting time," I hiss. "Get the fuck off me and let's do this."

Despite his excruciating pain, a hint of a smile appears on his shadowed face.

Chapter 20

The guy's a fucking lunatic.

As I flap my wings, soaring from left to right around the dragon's intimidating jaw, Ace stands in the parking lot, waving his arms above his head. He runs with a limp, and it's clear he's still in excruciating pain.

"Over here, you ugly beast!"

Is that all he has? Ugly beast? Ace is a gentleman, to say the least. If it were me down there, I'd be shouting all kinds of profanities.

Goddamn motherfucker.

Rotting piece of horseshit.

Fucking shit stain—

The dragon's jaw snaps shut, its three-foot-long incisor teeth inches away from my thigh.

I blast my wings downward to propel myself higher over the clouds.

Fuck.

That was way too close.

Realizing I'm flying close by, the dragon rolls its head back as if it doesn't have a spine and tries to catch me again. I fasten my grip around the sword Ace gave me and glare at the creature. It seems to do the same, its monstrous yellow eyes narrowing into slits the size of kayaks.

It seems like it's about to jump off the rooftop and chase me through the sky when at once, it seals its eyes and lets out a throaty cry. It raises its arm, revealing a bloody puncture wound in the soft side of its belly.

In the parking lot, Ace loads another arrow into his crossbow and aims it at the dragon's heart.

The elastic of his crossbow snaps and the sharp-tipped arrow comes whistling through the air.

But the moment it crashes into the dragon's chest, it shatters in two as if the dragon's scales are made of metal.

Shit. This isn't good.

Ace loads another arrow, but it won't do us any good. We're running out of time. The dragon's eyes turn on me. Widening its mouth again, it sends a fiery blast toward me. Although I fly away in time, the heat is so intense it burns my back.

We're pissing it off, and it's getting more and more aggressive.

If it doesn't bite off my head, I'll be fine, I tell myself.

With knees bent and wings expanded far on either side of me, I suck in a deep breath, preparing myself mentally. I've got one shot at this, so I can't fuck it—

Another fiery blast explodes beside me.

I'm out of time.

With my sword pointed straight ahead, I let out a hoarse cry and launch myself straight toward the dragon's face. I'm about to slice the blade through its neck when it opens its mouth as wide as possible, like a dog catching a treat midair.

It happens so fast I don't have the time to change my direction.

Fucking motherfucking shit.

It's too late. I'm going in.

Wincing, I crash headfirst against the dragon's tongue and tumble less than gracefully toward its throat. The impact is so forceful that my sword goes flying out of my hand and lands behind one of its massive plaque-encrusted molars.

"No, no, no," I shout in a panic.

I need that thing.

But suddenly, every muscle inside the dragon's mouth and throat contracts, sucking me toward the darkness at the back of its throat.

I'll be damned if I let this son of a bitch swallow me into its stomach acids.

In a panic, I extract my claws and stab them into the dragon's tongue. Speckles of blood splash onto my face as I puncture the muscle, but I'm not strong enough, and its tongue is too slimy. The dragon swallows again and I'm pulled back another several feet, my claws leaving scratch marks against the pink bubbly surface.

Then, something takes me by surprise… a deep rumble that feels a bit like an earthquake. Given the fact that I'm inside a dragon's mouth, I know it's anything but.

The air becomes hot—so hot that I can't catch my breath. Within a split second, a blinding light flashes all around me and searing hot flames explode out of the back of its throat. I've slipped far enough down its throat to avoid being touched, but I'm so close to the flames I'm afraid my face might melt off.

Wincing, I turn my face away and dig it into the slime of its tongue. My stomach contracts and I gag with my mouth closed and my cheeks ballooned.

When the fire blast stops at long last, I glance up and spot two holes at the back of the dragon's throat.

And here I thought dragons produced fire in their stomachs.

Thank the goddesses I ended up slipping down this far. Scorched Alexis wouldn't make a seductive succubus.

In a last desperate attempt, I extend my arm out toward the sword as if I'm going to miraculously obtain telekinesis abilities. To my dismay, the sword doesn't budge, and the next thing I know, I'm sliding down the beast's dark throat, my entire body drenched in hot slime.

Chapter 21

If I can throw a drunken tantrum in my apartment and destroy my walls, my floors, and my furniture, I can sure as hell make this dragon regret swallowing me.

The initial plan was to bring my sword down with me, but clearly, that didn't happen.

You see it all the time in movies; the hero gets swallowed by some giant monster, everyone thinks they're dead, and then *bam!* A sword bursts out of the dragon's chest or neck and the hero comes out unharmed.

How cool would that have been? I bet it would have impressed Ace.

I feel idiotic for even thinking about impressing that guy.

Alexis should never have to impress anyone.

The last time I felt this way was when I was a child and young Constantine—the most attractive lad in the village—reached for my hand.

But those days are nothing more than a distant memory. I'm a highly independent woman. Not once in my entire adult life have I ever felt the need to *impress* anyone, especially a man—well, anyone but Veerka. But with Veerka, everything feels different. I have this instinctive need to protect her. Ace doesn't need my protection, and if anything, he's throwing me off my game.

I'm aware it's related to him being an incubus, but the feeling still bothers me.

As I descend into the dragon's esophagus, I prepare my wrist blades, my teeth, and my six-inch wing claws. Then, as if possessed by a tornado, I spin myself in every direction imaginable, scratching, clawing, biting, stabbing, and tearing through any flesh I can reach.

The creature roars, the vibrations of its vocal cords reaching me as I fall. Hot blood spews onto my face, so I squint as I lash out, but I don't stop. No way am I reaching this thing's stomach acid. Who knows what's rotting in there? Bones and melted flesh?

I lose my momentum when the dragon jerks hard, no doubt panicking because its insides are being shred to pieces.

Good.

That's what it gets for fucking eating me.

With all my strength, I tear through its esophagus, hot slabs of fleshy skin drenching me in slime as I force my way out of the organ. Although difficult to slip out of the hole, I do so by grasping what seems to be a thick piece of muscle inside the dragon's throat.

With my wrist blades aimed up over my head, I dive headfirst through its neck as bits of muscles, tendons, and veins snap all around me. As I come blasting out into the sky, I grimace.

But it isn't the brightness of the sun that bothers me—it's the thick layer of bodily fluids dripping from my body. It's so thick that it weighs my wings down, making it difficult for me to flap. Every time I try, I lose control, along with several feet of altitude.

No matter how hard I try to shake off the dragon's blood and goo, it doesn't work. With a knot in my stomach, I spiral down at full speed toward the parking lot, my wings utterly useless.

I blink hard as the parking lot's asphalt gets closer and closer...

Well, this is gonna hurt.

It wouldn't be the first time I shatter every bone in my body. Pain, I can handle, but with everything that's going on right now, I don't have the luxury of time. Healing from such a severe injury typically takes me several days.

Fuck.

Submitting to my fate, I close my eyes and clench my jaw, twirling my body midair to aim my back at the ground. Despite my healing abilities, I always protect my face. What can I say? It's my money-maker. That, along with my chest.

Here goes nothing.

I brace for impact, prepared to feel excruciating pain explode throughout my entire body, but nothing happens. Am I still falling? Confused, I crack one eye open.

Around me is bright blue light forming what appears to be some protective capsule.

What's going on?

"Out of my way!" comes Rachel's voice.

The magical capsule disappears instantly, and I'm lying flat on my back, right next to an iguana with long yellow spikes, slits for eyes, and a small belly that expands with every labored breath.

What is that ugly thing?

Rachel comes bolting toward me and the iguana at full speed, the terrified expression on her face making me think she's running *away* from something.

"Oh, no!" she says the moment she reaches me.

"I'm okay—" I say, squeegeeing bloody slime off my face with my hands.

But Rachel doesn't even acknowledge me.

Instead, she bends over and scoops up the iguana, its massive tail dangling over her elbow. Her lip trembles like she's on the verge of crying. "You hurt him!"

My eyes almost pop out of my face. Is this kid for real? I sliced myself out of a fucking dragon, and all she can think about is some fucking lizard?

I'm about to ream her out when I notice the puncture wound on the iguana's throat.

174

Holy shit.

Is that the dragon?

Jumping up onto my feet, I rush toward Rachel. Meanwhile, Ace, Drax, and several other people I don't recognize form a crowd.

"Here, let me help," comes a boy's voice.

The guy, seemingly the same age as Rachel, steps forward and spreads his fingers over the iguana's neck. Soft green swirls spill out from his fingertips and engulf the iguana in Rachel's arms. The second the colorful magic disappears, the iguana's eyes enlarge and it shuts its mouth, the crease of it forming what resembles a smile.

Beaming, Rachel turns to the young male witch. "Wow, thank you!"

He smiles at her and offers a brief nod.

Is this actually happening? From where I'm standing, I did what was needed to protect myself, along with everyone else. And now *I'm* the bad guy for hurting the thing? It might be cute now, but it wasn't cute when its giant teeth were chomping down next to my thighs.

"Seriously?" I blurt, no longer able to contain myself. "I saved your lives."

"Actually—" Rachel says, but the witch nudges her in the ribs and she stops talking.

Biting my tongue, I turn to Ace, but he locks his fingers together and looks away. All that's missing is him whistling a tune.

"Did you turn it into a lizard, or was it a lizard

to begin with?" I ask, swallowing my resentment.

"It was a lizard first," says the witch.

The kid seems sweet, but after nearly getting my skin melted off inside the beast's stomach, I'm lacking a bit of patience. He must sense my irritation. Politely, he bows his head and folds his hands over his belly. "Thank you for your help. If you hadn't brought him back to the ground, I may not have gotten a clear shot."

"You did this?" I ask, pointing at the spiked creature.

Again, he nods.

I wouldn't peg him for a witch at all. He looks like your average teenage guy—tall and lanky, torn jeans, converse sneakers, shaggy chestnut hair, tanned skin, and a blue hoodie that looks like it hasn't been washed in weeks.

"So, if I hadn't pissed the dragon off in the first place, you would have had a clear shot."

He smirks, and it's obvious he doesn't want to piss *me* off.

I like this kid.

"What's done is done," he says. Awkwardly, he reaches toward his face and scratches the skin above his lip. That's when I see it—the ring.

"You're one of us," I say.

Surprised, his eyes dart to my hand, where, unlike him, I'm not wearing my ring.

Clearing my throat, I stick an open palm out at Rachel. She reaches into her pocket and hands me back my ring. I slide it back on.

"We're all on the same team," I say.

The kid hesitates, his big brown eyes rolling toward Drax, Riskus, and even Mr. Mushroom who keeps sniffing the iguana's hanging tail.

"They're with me," I say.

He doesn't argue. I'm certain he can tell that when I say something, I mean it. And if I say my people are trustworthy, he has no reason to question me.

"I can appreciate that," he says, "but they won't be allowed in the meeting."

Rachel frowns, possibly having realized she's not part of the ring club, either.

"What meeting?" I ask.

"The Battalion meeting taking place this evening."

He hesitates, his gaze searching Rachel and Drax. "They won't be able to attend."

"I'm aware," I say sharply. "But I can. So where is it?"

Without smiling, he throws his chin out at the grungy bar next to the motel's head office. "Meet me there at seven, and I'll show you the way."

CHAPTER 22

I'm not surprised that the only way into the meeting was through some magical portal enabled by the Battalion rings. Not that it matters. I've been around enough magic lately—I'm getting used to the whole portal thing.

Rachel wasn't happy about not joining us. She's made friends with Zane, the teenage male witch, and must want to impress him. Hey, I don't blame the kid. By the sounds of it, she doesn't have many friends, so this could be a great thing for her. But as much as she wants to contribute to this battle, there's no way she could have made it through the portal. Only those who wear the Battalion ring can pass through.

Poor girl.

She'll have to sit tight with Drax and the others until Ace and I get back.

The crowd is getting thicker by the minute.

Witches, fae, and a handful of vampires gather inside the open space, whispering about Zerachu, the Dark Hall, and the End of the Divide. It all makes sense to me now that the rebellion would include all races—not merely vampires. What was I thinking? Everyone is aware of vampire corruption, and everyone is affected. That means we all have our part to play, regardless of skin color, background, or magical abilities.

I gaze around the room at the low ceiling, the musty carpet, and the yellow walls. Small windows sit below the ceiling tiles, which tells me we're in a basement.

"This is outrageous!" shouts an old witch.

Then, the woman next to him paces in small circles. "Never in a million years..."

An enormous four-eyed demon steps between the two of them, and the woman stops pacing before bumping into his belly. "Talkin' about it ain't gonna fix nothing. We need to make a plan."

The old male witch glares up at him with a tight jaw engulfed in a ratty beard. "Would you shut your—" He stops himself and spins around before any more offensive words can come spilling out of his mouth.

It's difficult to imagine Devania allowing someone like *him* to be a part of the Battalion, but I'm willing to bet that panic is what's bringing out the worst in people.

Ace leans into me. "They aren't usually like this. They're scared."

Aren't usually like this? For Ace to say that means he's attended one of these meetings before.

How often do they occur? Does Devania make an appearance, too? Is it limited to San Halos and surrounding areas, or do people come here from all over the world? Given the fact that I walked through a portal to get here, there's a good chance I'm nowhere near San Halos anymore.

The room seems to contract as more and more people appear through the circle of bright green light. Some carry luggage, others cling to their wands.

"This is bad," comes a deep yet feminine voice.

I turn sideways to find a woman standing next to me with arms crossed over her frayed leather jacket. Down the side of her neck is a tattoo of a skull with a red rose in its mouth. She squints at the crowd with her black-outlined eyes, almost as if assessing the crowd's worthiness. But when she senses me watching her, her features soften.

I have that effect on people.

Turning to me, she pulls her long chestnut hair over one shoulder and takes me in... my mouth, my chest, my hips. If we weren't standing in a crowd full of unofficial heroes, I'd throw my Lure at her and drag her someplace quiet.

"I've never seen you before," she says, almost suggestively.

She doesn't smell like any demon I know—the only scent I'm getting off her is a sweet, fruity perfume, which means there's a good chance she's a witch.

I tilt my head to the right. "How unfortunate for you."

Hey, I get that I'm hot. Considering I chose this body, I can say that. I also know that I tend to attract attention without my Lure, but her response seems more impassioned than what I'm used to.

"You're a succubus," she says, matter-of-factly.

How did she figure me out so quickly? "I am."

Gnawing at her plump bottom lip, she gives me a full up-and-down. "You look like you need replenishing."

Is this happening? While I'm used to having feebles throw themselves at me even without my Lure, having someone approach me so nonchalantly while knowing full well what I am is new to me.

"I do," I say.

Without another word, she grabs my wrist and leads me around the crowd. I turn my head back in time to spot Ace watching us with a tense jaw.

Is he jealous? The guy barely even knows me. Not that it matters. I'm not passing up a good meal over someone else's feelings.

She leads me through an open door and into a small kitchenette. Ensuring no one is around to see us, she clicks her fingers and makes the wall next to the fridge swirl as if it's nothing more than wet paint floating in the air. She pulls me in and I wince. But much *unlike* drywall, the surface isn't hard, and

I slip right through as if the wall is made of water.

Does she expect me to do the same?

The passage leads us into another room—one much smaller that could be mistaken for a broom closet. The light above us hangs by an old wire, the dim bulb swaying from side to side. Around us are cardboard boxes covered in cobwebs, and beside them, more boxes.

Good thing I'm not a romantic.

I'm about to make some sarcastic remark about how talented she is at the romance game when she spins on her heels and her long wavy hair follows. Everything around me instantly fades. The only thing I can focus on now is my hunger.

"All right," she says, as if I'm wasting her time. "Let's do this."

I swallow hard, taken aback by her brazenness.

"You do understand what I am, don't you?" I ask.

Why am I even talking? I should get on with it.

She rolls her eyes and holds her hips like an impatient schoolteacher. "I know what I'm dealing with. This isn't my first rodeo."

Maybe not for her, but it is for me.

Why the hell would anyone specifically seek out succubi sex? I mean, don't get me wrong—my sex is worth chasing time and time again. But not all succubi are like me in the sense that they let their victims survive.

Most don't.

So how can this woman be so bold? How does

she know that I won't drain her like a swimming pool before winter?

Sighing, she unbuttons her jeans, pulls off her jacket, and slips off her T-shirt. Without even bothering to look at me, she finishes undressing and stares at me as if to say, *Are we gonna do this, or what?*

In the middle of her belly is a pentagram belly ring, but I don't focus on that for long. My eyes drop toward her perfect naked body and my claws snap out.

With shoulders hunched forward like a predator on the verge of pouncing, I take a step forward. Now, I'm hungry.

As I prepare my meal, she lets out a few loud moans. Halfway through, I grab her by the hair and pull hard enough for her to wince in pain. "Shut up."

There's no telling how thin these walls are, and the last thing I want is for the entire underground rebellion to eyeball us when we come stepping back into the main hall.

Although she stops shouting, something else happens.

Something weird.

Right in the middle of our steamy moment, she murmurs a bunch of jumbled nonsense.

Shit... I broke her.

Doesn't matter. Now's my chance. I'm about to flip her around and enjoy my meal when I realize what's going on: she's speaking in Latin. Why does that matter? Witches speak in Latin when they're...

Are you shitting me? Is she casting a fucking spell?

I stop what I'm doing and grab her by the back of the neck, pinning her face against the wall.

"What the fuck?" she says, her mouth partially squished. "Why'd you stop?"

I wasn't born yesterday—far from it. First, witches use Latin as their primary language for performing spells; everyone knows that. And if they aren't speaking in Latin, they're letting out random words that sound a lot like it.

Second, I've heard of witches like her. They use the intensity of orgasms to cast some of the most powerful spells ever known to witches. Her use of succubus sex means that whatever spell she's trying to cast is unlike anything I've seen before.

How could I have missed this?

She glares at me from the corner of her eye as large squiggly veins protrude from her temples. She's fuming, which is either because I cut her pleasure short or because I cut her spell short. Or maybe a bit of both.

Who cares?

I'm the one who should be pissed. I was about to feed and she distracted me. Who is she, and what's her deal?

"Why are you trying to perform sex magic?" I ask, my fingers still wrapped around her neck.

Breathing out hard, she tries to push me off.

"What do you care? You're a succubus. Everyone knows succubus demons don't give a shit about anyone else but themselves."

Rude.

Is that what people think of me?

Well, who gives a shit?

I push her harder into the wall until a hairline crack splits down the drywall. "You gonna talk, or would you prefer to get your vocal cords crushed?"

Her face is now three shades darker than it was seconds ago.

"Okay, okay," she mumbles.

Shoving her one last time, I let it go.

She grabs at the back of her head, then reaches for her inflamed cheek.

"My name's... my name's Cassidy."

I don't give a shit about your life story. Get to the point.

I should feel bad for hurting her, but I don't. Being used by someone is something I don't tolerate. If there's one thing I hate more than being lied to, it's being made to feel like a moron. The stunt she pulled made me feel both, not to mention frustrated beyond belief.

How did I not see this coming? I've had demons approach me to get a taste of my sex, but not like this. It wasn't the sex she wanted—it was the climax. I should have sensed what was going on.

"Get to the point, Cassidy."

She stretches her neck sideways, and that's

when I notice it.

Her hand.

Where's her ring? The only people who should be present in this place are Devania's people—those she's vetted through a series of trials to determine their trustworthiness.

I should know. I had to go through all that shit myself.

I clench a fist, prepared to pin her to the wall again, but she must know what I'm thinking. At once, she raises her hands, palms out, to her crimson face. "Easy. I'm not a bad guy."

"Then where's your ring?" I say sharply.

"It's complicated."

"Then uncomplicate it for me."

She sighs as if the story she's about to tell me is too farfetched to believe.

"There's a new spell going around," she says. "It mimics that ring's magic." She points at my hand, where my Battalion ring sits. "Basically, the spell lets me in on the meetings. Some people are even replicating the actual ring. If I'd had more time, I might have done that, but I didn't."

I narrow my glare to get her to talk faster.

"Listen, I'm not here to cause any trouble. I only wanted inside the meeting to find a succubus."

I'm not sure what's throwing me off the most—that Devania's rings can no longer be trusted as proof of alliance, or that this witch specifically sought out a succubus to cast some outrageous spell.

She opens her mouth before I can threaten her. "Word has it that these meetings are all about inclusivity. I tried my luck at meeting succubi at the Dark Hall, but then, well, everything went to shit. That's when I found out about the Battalion."

How would she even know about the Battalion?

Her protruding brows meet in the middle of her forehead. "Why do you look so shocked? Haven't you noticed what's going on? There's chaos everywhere. People are panicking. Whoever's running this underground thing is a quack if they think their big secret is still a secret. You can't trust anyone. There will always be traitors."

I don't want to believe her, but deep down, I know she's right.

Everything's gone to shit, and if Zerachu herself can be kidnapped and taken out of the Dark Hall, the bad guys have most definitely found a way to infiltrate Devania's Battalion.

"If you knew about the Battalion, why not become a member?"

"I tried, but it turns out I'm too hung up on my own needs."

So, she let the Cerberus maul the girl. For what?

"Say I believe you," I retort. "What spell were you trying to cast? What is it you want so badly? Because if you aren't one of the bad guys, what the hell are you doing chasing after so much power in the middle of a Battalion meeting?"

She looks away, and I can't tell if she's ashamed or heartbroken.

"I'm trying to cast a resurrection spell," she mumbles.

I'm about to slap her across the face, so instead, I bite the tip of my tongue until it hurts.

"I don't need to hear your speech," she says, no doubt sensing my disapproval.

"Good," I say. "I'm glad you already know you're an idiot."

"He was my one and only," she says.

A lover.

I should have known.

Admittedly, I do feel a bit sorry for her. I know what it's like to get hung up on wanting to bring a loved one back from the dead. I considered it more times than once with Jamal, and with several other people from my past, but everyone knows resurrection spells don't work. At least not in the way people want them to.

"It wouldn't be *him*," I say.

She knows this—that's why she looks like she's been caught cheating on an exam.

"I know," she finally breathes. Her lower lip trembles, so I grab her by the face.

"Listen to me," I say.

Minutes ago, Cassidy looked like she didn't give a shit about anything other than getting her lover back. But now, as I stare her cold in the face, it's obvious she's terrified and desperate for help.

"You need to stop chasing after the dead. When your time on Earth is up, you'll see him again, you hear me?"

With her cheeks deflated between my fingers, she scoffs. "How would you know anything about the afterlife?"

"Isn't it obvious? I'm immortal. Well, my body is. I've been thrown out of it more times than I can count, and I can assure you that there's more to life than this physical bullshit."

A glimmer of hope sparkles in her eyes, so I let go of her face.

"Now, will you stop with the sex magic and live the only mortal life you have?"

With watery eyes, she nods.

Would you look at that? I helped someone despite my anger. Surprisingly, it doesn't feel too bad. Clearing my throat to rid the awkward silence, I stiffen my stance. "Now that I've given you something, I want something in return."

"Anything," she says.

Chapter 23

Ace looks as pissed off as I was when I caught Cassidy casting a spell midorgasm.

He watches me from behind the tip of his nose. "Something's wrong."

"What?" I brush my hair over one shoulder—something I always do when I'm lying or trying to cover something up. "What do you mean?"

Does he know what happened? Is he fishing for information? I'm afraid to tell him what I've discovered. Now that I know Battalion rings can be faked, who do I trust? What if Ace is one of the traitors?

"Where is she?" someone shouts.

"Maybe they got to her!"

"Shut your trap!"

"What's going on?" I ask him, thankful for the distraction.

Without looking at me, he says, "Devania should have been here by now."

After a prolonged silence, a dwarf shoves his way through the crowd, his pointed elbows jabbing anything that gets in his way. His labored breathing makes it difficult to differentiate the sound of his steps from the air coming out of his mouth.

"Outta the way," he grumbles.

He's so short he that he blends into the crowd, but as everyone steps aside to let him pass, he comes into view. With dark green wrinkled skin and long pointed ears, there's no mistaking what he is. I understand why feebles portray dwarves as these hideous creatures. This guy matches the description with the wiry white hairs coming out of his ears and a long hook for a nose. If I were to describe dwarves through comparison, I'd say they were the spawn of an ogre and a goblin—two creatures I'd never want to see fornicating.

With a loud huff, he pulls himself up onto a chair to be level with everyone else.

"Attention, everyone," he says, his rumbly voice carrying over everyone's heads.

To my surprise, the crowd stops bickering and listens with anticipation. Why wouldn't they? Devania's not here, and it's obvious that these people want answers.

He offers what appears to be a smile someone paid him to give—a crack full of yellow squares for teeth.

"There have been complications," he says.

The crowd blows up again.

"What kind of complications?"

"What's the Council Elders doing about this?

Consequences are in order!"

"Oh, shut your trap, ya rusted lug nut. Nothin' is in order, don't ya see that? The council's fallin' apart!"

"Who told you this?"

"Where is she getting her information?"

And these people are supposed to be worthy? Maybe I'm not so bad after all.

"Enough!" comes the dwarf's voice. It blasts across the room louder than anyone else's, the sheer power of it causing everyone's hair to wave in its wind.

His glossy yellow eyes roll from side to side, inspecting the group. It's like he knows there are traitors among us, but he's afraid to let the news spill. If he does, chaos will unravel.

"Hey," comes Rachel's voice.

Holy shit. My plan worked.

The dwarf goes on to talk about something, but I tune him out. Spinning around, I wrap a protective arm around Rachel as if trying to protect her from the paparazzi. If she's seen by someone who knows she isn't part of the Battalion, there's no telling what will happen.

Ace's brows come so close together you'd think an invisible force was compressing his face. "What the hell is going on?" he whispers sharply.

The glare I give him is enough to shut him up. The last thing we need is for everyone's panic to shift our way.

"Keep cool," I hiss back. "I brought her here."

He keeps his mouth shut and watches us, a strange look in his eyes.

Jerking my head sideways, I lead Rachel as far away from Ace as I can, which isn't far. I want to trust the guy—I really, *really* do—but my motto has always been guilty until proven innocent. I've seen enough con artists in my life to know that trust is as precious as pink diamonds.

Right now, the only people I trust are Drax and Rachel. I'd say I trust Mr. Mushroom, but even some days I wonder if he's more than what he lets on.

The moment we step away from everyone, Rachel's eyes light up and she wiggles her hand in front of my face, her fake ruby ring glistening under the shitty basement lights. "Cassidy said you sent her. How'd you meet her?" Rachel says.

"Let's say I have my ways," I say, not wanting to get into the details of my situation with Cassidy the witch.

"She was super cool," Rachel says. "She made it look so easy." She grins at her ring again like it's the most precious thing she owns. "You can't even tell it's not—"

With my fingers still wrapped around her shoulder, I squeeze hard and she stops talking. This room is filled with so many different races that there's bound to be someone in here with ears like an owl.

"Listen," I whisper. "We can't talk here. I need

you to pay attention to what's going on. I get the feeling we're going to need your help."

Her posture stiffens and she beams at me. I get it. Everyone wants to feel like they're needed or valued, and Rachel's no exception. It doesn't help that since I met her, not once have I made her feel important. All I've done is tell her how much of an amateur she is and how she'll get hurt. I might not be happy about how things started, but it's become obvious that Zerachu's blood runs through her.

The kid's got a gift.

"We don't know," the dwarf says grimly. "No one can track her."

Shit. What did I miss? I move toward Ace, who looks like he's about to vomit. He gives me a look that says, *This is really bad*, which leads me to believe that maybe he isn't a bad guy, after all.

He *is* one of the good guys, isn't he?

"What are we supposed to do?" someone asks.

An eerie silence fills the room, and every breath taken sounds like a gasp in contrast.

"Devania is looking into this," the dwarf says, "but until she discovers who is behind all of this, she will remain in hiding."

I lean toward Ace. "What did I miss?"

With wide eyes locked on the fat dwarf at the front, he says, "Zerachu's being held captive somewhere, and no one knows where. The spell that was cast inside the Dark Hall was a form of blood magic. Her blood. Even the Council of Elders can't figure this one out. But it wasn't Zerachu who cast it, which doesn't make much sense."

Rachel smiles up at me, looking a bit goofy amid the gloom and panic in the room. Thankfully, Ace doesn't see her, and I manage to frown at her in time to get her to wipe that slick smile off her face.

I get that she's excited—she's related to Zerachu, and she and I are the two people in the room privy to this information. In short, Rachel is the only one who can save her great-aunt, and ultimately, save the world.

Wow, that sounded dramatic.

But it's true... and it's huge.

That's what she said.

Although I trust that she's a mighty witch, things are getting dangerous. When even the Elders can't fix something, things are bad. *Really bad.* That's what happens when witches use blood magic.

I'm glad we have the same blood standing right here in this room, but how the hell does a kid stand a chance against something this crazy?

I swallow hard, feeling bile bubble in the pit of my stomach. Am I anxious, or withdrawing from alcohol?

"You're telling us we can't go out into view?" someone shouts.

The round dwarf nods slowly. "The spell is worldwide. Humans can see your true form."

"But vampires are free to walk about as they

please," a Gorton cuts in. "This was clearly orchestrated by them."

"Yes, group us all into one..." comes a somber voice.

At the far back corner stands a vampire with arms crossed over his belly, a long leather jacket that hangs right above his ankles, and a sour look on his face that tells me he doesn't put up with being labeled.

"Anthony, you know I didn't mean—" says the Gorton.

Anthony the vampire raises a white hand—a gesture meant to signify, *don't waste your breath*—and the Gorton's mouth becomes a flat line.

"We don't have proof of anything," the dwarf says. He scratches his dark, wrinkled skin and sighs toward the ceiling. The guy reminds me of a police chief who's spent too long in his position. "All I know is that static fae must remain in hiding."

By static, he means demons who can't conceal their true selves. Luckily for me, I look human unless I choose to reveal myself. People like Drax, however, are always their demon selves. Magic protects them from feebles and now, that's been tampered with.

"Well..." comes a familiar voice. "Many of us can still walk among humans."

Out from the crowd comes the teenage witch from earlier—the kid who helped us out with the dragon.

"Zane," Rachel breathes.

Zane's dark eyes roll toward her. He hesitates, his lips partially open, but then turns his attention back toward the crowd.

Shit.

He knows she isn't supposed to be in here. Hopefully, he likes her enough to not rat her out.

"Until the Elders figure out how to disable this spell," he says simply, "our brothers and sisters will have to fight in the shadows."

By brothers and sisters, I assume he's referring to any static demon within the Battalion.

Everyone nods slowly, almost entranced, as if Devania were the one speaking. Who is this kid and why is everyone suddenly showing so much respect?

"The Council of Elders is searching for the *Book of Origin* and the Heart of Danu as we speak. They've asked for our help to keep our kind away from the humans."

The energy in the room shifts.

For the first time, I see a group of soldiers prepared to fight for a cause—not a crowd of panicked shadow dwellers.

Out from the crowd comes a tall, dark-skinned man with white eyes and pointed ears. "We will spread the word among our people."

A dark faerie.

Beside him are three others—one male and two females. They nod without saying a word, their piercing eyes searching the room.

Dark faeries get a bad rap, but what people don't understand is that they aren't all evil. A lot of them are good, but their magic is badass and often deadly.

Everyone knows not to piss off a dark faerie, which makes having them on our side invaluable.

Zane places a solid fist over his chest and lowers his head—a gesture meant to signify *thank you*, or *good luck*.

"We will fight to the death," comes a deep, yet feminine voice.

She steps forward, her plated chest gleaming, and wraps her fingers around her sword's hilt. Her hair, long and braided, hangs over one shoulder down to her waist. I don't even have to smell her to know what she is—an Amazonus demon.

Sometimes referred to as Amazons in Greek mythology, Amazonus demons have been around for centuries. Although they don't possess any magic, they're bold, courageous, and possess strength comparable to that of ten feebles, making them ideal soldiers. Behind her stands another dozen women in metal plated armor, their chins level with the floor and their fearless eyes fixated straight ahead.

Again, Zane touches his chest and bows.

More and more shadow dwellers step forward, offering their skills and specialties to the cause.

Ace glances sideways at me, likely wondering

the same thing I am: what do we as sex demons have to offer the world other than a good time?

Biting my lip, I stare back at him. Am I seriously pondering whether to offer my strength as an act of heroism? This isn't like me. My gaze shifts toward my Battalion ring.

What the hell did you do to me, Devania?

Is this thing laced with *Let's fix the world* magic?

My mind wanders back to the dragon's rancid internal organs and how I tore out of that thing like it was nothing. Okay—it wasn't *nothing*. It was disgusting, and it sucked up much of my energy.

But I managed it, which means my strength is something I can offer. So why isn't Ace saying anything? And why is he staring at me? The guy's proven himself to be stronger than me, yet he stands there looking like a sheep... like someone prepared to obey any order I give.

And I haven't even used my Lure on the guy.

How could someone who can teleport with a click of their fingers turn to me—a drunk—for guidance?

You may have fallen victim to feeble weaknesses, but you are not weak.

The voice is my own, but the words sound like something that Alice, my doll, would say to me. Is she in my head? Or, is she still following me?

Probably.

I listen to my gut, or Alice—whoever is responsible for my little inner pep talk. Deep down,

I know I'm a force to be reckoned with. Somewhere along the way after Jamal was killed, I allowed grief to consume me. I'm still hurting inside—I miss Jamal more than anything—but what I've become is something I'm not proud of, and I know for a fact that if he's watching me, he's no doubt disappointed in what I've become.

"I have an idea," I say, pulling my shoulders back.

Ace widens his stance and stiffens.

"Give me your ring," I order.

He arches a brow, no doubt thinking I've lost my mind. We were transported here through a portal, which means the one way back is through another portal. Without the ring, there's no way back. Well, unless he's one of the traitors.

God… gorgeous and brilliant.

"Come on," I say. "Hand it over."

Although confused, he does as told and places it in the palm of my hand.

Behind us, a line has already formed, and one by one, people walk through the exit portal. I grab his arm and force my way toward the front of the line. "Excuse me. Sorry. Family emergency."

A few oomphs and umphs come from people's mouths as I push my way through, but no one tells me to back off.

"Rayne, what the hell—" Ace tries, but before he can argue, I push him as hard as I can into the portal.

I realize it's a risk and possibly a stupid one, at that. But I need to be sure.

Fiery red sparks burst out of the portal, followed by a loud crackling noise similar to that of a forgotten fork inside a microwave. Before I can react, Ace shoots across the room and over everyone's heads. He lands hard against the chief dwarf, and together, they tumble against the back wall.

Shrieks and shouts fill the room as people run to the back.

What a relief. I mean... Wow, that must have hurt.

"Oh my goddess," I shout with a dumbed-down, ditsy voice. "Sorry. So sorry." I rush across the room like I'm stepping on hot coals and offer the crowd a guilty smile. The looks I'm getting range from, *Is he okay?* to *What the fuck just happened?*

I raise Ace's ring to my face and stretch a fake grin. "Silly me. His ring was dirty and I wanted to clean it for him. Then I find out my brother's gone missing—" I fan my face. "Wow. I'm so sorry. My mind is all over the place."

Grunting, Ace gets up but shoots his arms out to maintain balance, his focus wandering around the room.

"You're okay," I say, now letting out a ridiculous laugh. "Walk it off."

I grab him by the arm and help him back to the portal. He's too dazed now, but he'll interrogate me soon enough and ask me if I need professional help.

Still smiling awkwardly at everyone, I slip his ring back on and flash Rachel a frown that translates to, *Let's go.*

She hurries to the front with us, and together, we all jump through.

Chapter 24

Rachel paces across the remains of the motel room as if trying to decipher some advanced calculus equation. She rubs her chin, scratches the back of her head, and then stands with her hands clutching her hips. "You realize there's no guarantee this'll work, right?"

I glance sideways at Ace sitting at the edge of the bed with an ice pack on his cheek.

He's pissed off, but it had to be done.

Wincing apologetically, I say, "I had to be sure.

"I know," he grumbles. "I would've done the same thing."

Rachel glares at us as if she's being paid by the minute to be here. "Hello?"

I sigh. "I know it isn't certain, Rachel, but you're the only one who has *something* that belongs to Zerachu."

She doesn't seem convinced. Why would she? This whole situation is a mess. I genuinely believe that the one person powerful enough to take down whoever did this is Zerachu. The Council of Elders is almighty, sure—but they don't know what goes on in the Dark Hall. That area is Zerachu's domain, and although she might be a bit of a whack job at times, she's the one person I wouldn't want to cross.

There's a reason the Great Witch is missing. Whoever did this knows she's a threat, which means we have to find her. And since no one can get back into the Dark Hall—I wish I'd known this before leaving—it's impossible to use one of her belongings to cast a location spell.

What I'm asking Rachel is so insane it just might work.

"So, do I have to take it out of me, or what?"

Drax doesn't look impressed, but I can tell he knows this is the only way.

"A bit," I say, handing Rachel one of my knives.

She takes it reluctantly and lets it hover over her left palm.

"I don't understand," Ace says, stopping Rachel before she applies pressure. "Why is she the one doing this?"

No one says anything, which is explanation enough. With eyes doubled in size, he gapes at Rachel. "You're related to—"

Rachel nods. "Apparently. So, am I doing this, or what? I do want to point out that this is some serious stuff. Once the portal opens, I don't think we should leave it open."

Ace stretches his swollen jaw and something

pops. "Rachel's right. I've seen someone create a blood portal once in my life, and the result, well... Let's say it wasn't a success."

"What's that supposed to mean?" Drax asks.

Behind him, Mr. Mushroom barks like he understands what we're talking about.

"Things don't always go as planned," I say. "But what choice do we have? The world is about to go to shit. I can guarantee you that the war has already started—"

"About that..." Ace says, sounding like he's withholding some big dark secret.

He may very well be, so I give him a stern look that translates to, I *don't have all day.*

"I overheard a few people talking during the Battalion meeting. The Council of Elders will attempt to cast an Interruptu spell."

Everyone in the room gasps, including me, which makes me feel like a total moron. "That's impossible."

He shakes his head. "I know it sounds insane, but this could change everything."

Rachel, still standing awkwardly with my blade in her palm, grimaces at us like we're speaking in another language. "What is that?"

"It pauses all feeble life," I say. "Every feeble on Earth gets placed into this isolation realm and when they return, they have no idea what happened to them."

"Well—" Drax says.

I roll my eyes. "The Council of Elders will never admit it, but they use the spell on certain individuals for unknown reasons. Some of these people have come forward with unusual marks on them, claiming they've been abducted by aliens."

"Can you blame them?" Drax says. "That's pretty invasive."

I swat the air in front of my face. "Who cares about privacy? That's not my point. I've never heard of the council being able to pull this off *worldwide*."

"Doesn't mean it's never happened," Ace says.

"Well, it hasn't in the last thousand years," I say. "Sorry to burst your bubble, but there's no way they'll pull it off."

"Still," Ace says. "It's a possibility. If we wait a while longer and the Council of Elders gets feebles out of our way—"

"It isn't happening," I cut him off. "And we can't rely on some miracle to make this easier for us. We need to stop whoever stole the book and the amulet before things get out of hand. The longer we wait, the worse things will get."

He tightens his lips.

Loud crunching fills the room, and everyone turns to look at Drax sitting on the bed with chips falling out of his mouth. "Hold up," Drax says, bits of chip flakes bursting into the air. "Why are we the ones doing this? The Council of Elders has its own army."

I point at Rachel with my nose. "But we have

her."

"Why didn't you tell the Battalion people, or whatever they're called?" Drax asks. But then he catches a glimpse of Rachel's fake ring and snaps his fingers. "Oh, I get it. Don't know who you can trust, right? For all we know, someone'll kidnap her and kill her to stop her from—"

"Drax," I hiss, and he stops talking.

His yellow eyes dart at Rachel. "Sorry, kid."

Rachel doesn't seem too bothered by it. From where I'm standing, it looks like she's ready and willing to give this a shot.

I pause, my stare lingering on the carpet floor. If only I could get ahold of Veerka. She's the one who sent me on this wild goose chase to begin with. So where is she now? Is she even on our side? If she isn't, why send me to the Battalion? It doesn't make sense. I'm surprised that this is the first time I think about her in hours, which I suppose makes sense given the fact that a dragon swallowed me and all.

"Are you ready?" I ask.

Rachel nods.

"Once I go in, close the portal. So long as I can get to Zerachu, we'll be able to get out."

"What?" Ace says. "You're the one going in?"

My eyes narrow on him. Is he an idiot? Who else is supposed to go in? Rachel may be the one opening the portal, but no way in hell am I letting her go in there. There's no telling what's waiting on the other side, which means the right candidate is someone who knows how to defend themselves.

"I'll go," he says.

I scoff, though I don't mean to. "I don't need a hero, Ace. I'm a strong, independent woman who's quite capable—"

Something slithers around my ankles and I let out a high-pitched shriek. The moment I jump backward, I realize it's the iguana from earlier. Well, the dragon.

"What the hell is that thing doing in here?" I snap.

"Leave Spike alone," Rachel says, bending down to pick him up.

"Spike," I repeat. "How original."

She pets the little spikes on the lizard's head and its eyes turn into black lines.

"You plan on keeping that thing?" I ask.

She scratches him between the eyes. "For now."

I'm about to say something mean, so instead, I wiggle a finger at the blade she's holding. "Let's get this over with."

Chapter 25

The portal twirls like a cyclone, its bloodred and majestic purple flashes mixing so perfectly it's making me want ice cream. I'm thinking the colors have something to do with the fact that it's related to blood magic, but I can't be certain. The room fills with a loud hum—a sound that could easily be mistaken for a nearby helicopter.

Preparing myself for the worst, I offer Ace a brief nod. I'm not afraid for my safety; I'm afraid I'll get lost and won't make my way back to Veerka and Mr. Mushroom. Okay, the rest of the gang, too. It wouldn't be the first time I get transported through another dimension only to return five years later.

What if Rachel fucked up? What if her portal *does* lead into another dimension? I made it clear that I need to remain on this Earth, but vocalizing my concerns doesn't change her abilities.

I step toward the portal, its sheer power causing my hair to flow behind me. Everyone else takes a step back like I'm about to step into a bomb.

Thanks, guys. Real comforting.

"Where you headed?" comes a familiar voice.

I spin around, my hair webbing my entire face. When I move it out of the way, my eyes land on Zane. With his back against the half-torn wall, he smirks arrogantly at the portal, and then at us.

"How the hell did you get in here?" I ask.

He gives me a one-shoulder shrug and then gazes up at the missing roof. Obviously, that's not how he got in, but he seems to be amused that he caught us all off guard.

More than likely, he teleported. He is a witch, after all.

"This doesn't concern you," I say sharply.

I don't mean to come across as a bitch, but I don't know the kid. He can't know what we're doing. Surprisingly, my tone doesn't faze him. Uncrossing his arms, he pushes himself into a standing position and walks toward us. The portal continues to twirl, creating little creases across his clothing.

Inspecting Rachel's creation, he says, "This looks like a blood portal."

Finally, some emotion on his face. His jaw loosens, and he turns to Rachel. "How did you pull this off?"

She looks at me, and when I shake my head, she doesn't respond. Although I like the kid, I don't approve of the way he sneaked up on us, especially when we're in the middle of something both private and dangerous.

He throws his chin out at Rachel. "I saw that you managed to enter the Battalion meeting, and I had to figure out what you were up to." As if suddenly possessed, he wrinkles his forehead and his brows meet above the bridge of his nose. With that furious look still on his face, he flattens his palms and makes two massive fireballs appear. "Did you take my mother?" he shouts.

I'm too shocked to say anything, and by how quiet the room's gotten, I'm thinking I'm not the only one.

"Answer me!"

Rachel takes a step back. Ace steps in front of her with his chest puffed out and his wings expanded.

Hot and protective... Focus, Alexis.

"What the hell are you talking about?" I say.

The calmness in my voice seems to provoke him. He makes his fireballs double in size and raises one higher than the other, prepared to launch it at me. Rachel's portal disappears in a flash.

Goddamn it.

Unable to contain myself, I laugh. I don't mean to, but is this kid trying to make us believe that Zerachu is his mother? I can't imagine that woman being with a man. She gives me that don't-fuck-with-me butch lesbian vibe.

"Pretending to be Zerachu's son won't get you anywhere," I say, extracting my claws.

If this kid wants a fight, he'll get one. I'm not

typically one to hit anyone under the age of eighteen, but he's asking for it.

The sound of Zerachu's name makes his fireballs disappear. "Zerachu?"

What the hell is going on here? What am I missing?

Clearing his throat, he composes himself as if the fireball threat never happened. "You don't know who I am, and with how confused you all appear to be, I realize now that you aren't the bad guys."

You think? Jackass.

"No, we aren't," I say. "So who the hell are you and what does your mother have to do with us?"

He elevates his chin as if prepared to tell us he's from a royal bloodline. "I'm Devania's son."

Okay, I wasn't expecting that one.

He stares at the ground. "She went missing when the Great Witch disappeared. No one's announcing it. They're afraid it might cause panic among the Battalion."

I sigh at the cloudy sky above us. "You have got to be kidding me."

"If you aren't one of the bad guys, why did you open up a blood portal?" he asks.

I don't want to tell this kid who Rachel is, but it's obvious that all he wants to do is find his mother. And if I don't tell him what's going on, he might refuse to leave. I'm all for using lethal force if necessary, but if I kill Devania's kid, I won't be around for long.

"First of all," I say, "you made us lose the portal. Thanks a lot, jack—"

Drax clears his throat to keep me in line.

"We're trying to find Zerachu," I say.

Zane furrows his brows. "How does that explain the blood portal? The only way you'd be creating a blood portal to find Zerachu is if—" And then, as if just now realizing he needs oxygen to live, his eyes widen and he twirls on his heels. "Someone in this room is related to the Great Witch?"

Rachel's stare lingers on me again, and this time, I nod as a way of giving her my approval.

"She's my great-aunt," Rachel says.

"Grandaunt, technically," I correct.

She gives me a sour look. "Whatever. It's the same thing. She's my grandmother's sister."

Zane smiles—a smug look that makes me wonder if he's even surprised. The only way a blood portal can be created is by someone who possesses the blood in question. If he's a witch, he should have known that. Maybe Devania has been too busy saving the world to teach her kid about magic.

And that's when it hits me. If Zane is the son of Devania, how did he become a witch? She's a Ukrisse demon, capable of morphing into any form, which would make him a hybrid.

"Devania isn't a witch," I say boldly.

Taken aback by my words, he turns to me and grimaces as if to say, *What's your point?*

"How did you turn out to be a one?"

"My father," he says coldly. "If you even want to call him that."

"Bad relationship?" Ace cuts in.

"He abandoned us a long time ago. I don't understand why you're interrogating me when you guys are the ones with a fake Battalion ring and a blood portal."

The kid has a point.

I'm about to ask him whether his ring is fake but I realize this would be a stupid thing to do. He's Devania's son—of course, it isn't fake. And even if it were, it's not like he'd admit to it. Besides, why would he have gone through all the trouble of taking us into the Battalion meeting?

I need to work on my trust issues.

"Let me help," he says. "Maybe my mom is being held captive with Zerachu."

I want to argue, but I can't. Finding both of them would be an absolute miracle right about now. The world needs Zerachu's magic, and the Battalion needs Devania's leadership.

"What do you have to offer?" I ask.

He points his chin at Rachel. "I'll go with her and ensure she remains safe."

I scoff. "I'm the one going. Do you honestly think I'd let—"

"You?" he asks, knitting his brows.

Is he trying to insult me? Does he not think me capable enough to handle a few bad guys? Okay, I might be downplaying it. For all I know, an entire army is positioned around Rachel's great-aunt. That is, if she's even still alive.

"You can't enter a blood portal on your own," he says.

This is news to me. "What are you talking about?"

"It's Rachel's blood, which means she has to be the one to go through. You can go with her, but not without her. And if you do accompany her, who's staying behind to fight? It's clear that fighting is your strength."

It's difficult to be angry at someone who compliments you.

I glance up at Ace, who appears as uncertain as me.

"Let me go with her," Zane says. "I'll ensure she's safe."

My eyes narrow on him. "A minute ago, you didn't even know who was related to Zerachu despite knowing Rachel created the portal." I extract my wrist blades. "What kind of games are you playing?"

He calmly shakes his head. "I'm playing no game, I assure you. I've heard of powerful sorcerers creating blood portals on behalf of other people... It's only that I've never seen it done. I'm putting myself on the line by trusting you."

Still glowering at him, I take in a long breath. "Okay, then why haven't you created your own blood portal to find your mother?"

He smirks. "I'm not *that* powerful."

Rachel beams, and I hope this won't go to her head.

On one hand, I don't like the idea of her going blindly through some portal with a guy we barely know. On the other hand, he's a witch, and if there's one thing better than a witch, it's two of them.

"I want her back in one piece," I say, jabbing my finger in front of his face.

Rachel looks at me like I'm an embarrassing mom, and that's when it hits me.

Rachel's mom. Surely, she's realized by now that Rachel's clone is precisely that—a clone.

"Rachel, how do you know your mom hasn't figured out the clone thing?"

She flicks her wrist at me. "I have a safeguard in place. If she figures it out, the clone sends me a signal."

"A signal?" I ask. "As in a magical telepathic message?"

She scrunches her nose and whips out her cell phone. "Um... A text."

Now I *definitely* feel like the embarrassing mom.

Zane tightens his lips, no doubt fighting the urge to laugh.

Teenagers.

I wave impatiently. "Create the portal again, will you?"

I realize I'm making it sound like it's as easy as

baking premade cookies when in reality, it drains a great deal of Rachel's energy. She still looks depleted from her first blood portal. I hope she has enough strength to go at it again.

Rubbing her palms together, she says, "Okay everyone, step back," and a powerful gust of wind sweeps through what's left of our motel room.

CHAPTER 26

Watching the portal close behind Rachel is the most difficult thing I've had to do in a while. It makes me want to chug back a bottle of tequila, but for her sake, I won't do it. I'm worried like hell that she won't make it back, but I can't focus on that.

She's doing her job. Ace and I need to do ours.

"You okay?" Ace asks.

I turn to look at both him and Drax, and Drax quickly avoids eye contact. He knows I hate getting emotional and so he does me the honor of pretending I have no feelings.

"I'm fine," I lie.

The truth is, I'm freaking out inside. I fucking hate uncertainty and I especially hate it when it concerns someone I care about. I also hate the fact that I give a shit about that little brat. This wasn't supposed to happen, yet somehow, she wormed her way into our dysfunctional family.

Ace loads his weapon belt, clipping on a pistol and two knives. He slips a sword into a long sheath. "Listen, if you need time—" he says, but I don't let him finish.

Moving at the speed of modern internet—quickly, in case that was misinterpreted—I grab him by the collar of his cotton shirt, march him backward across the room, and push him right through the wall. Dust explodes around us and a support beam snaps in two as we enter his old room—the one Rachel unknowingly led me into hours ago.

I throw him onto his bed. "Take off your pants."

He doesn't argue and quickly unbuttons them and tears them off. Beneath them are clean white boxer briefs that are form-fitting and quite flattering. I tear off my clothes, then scratch those boxers right off of him.

He winces as my claws draw blood, but he doesn't seem to mind.

Without giving him any time to ask what's going on, I start prepping my meal.

Both of our wings expand on either side of us the moment it starts, and I throw my head back as a feeling of absolute ecstasy runs through my veins.

But I need more. He must sense it. Using his wings, he pushes himself upward and spins me around onto my back. He's so strong, and muscular. I think my heart might stop.

His skin glistens as sweat seeps through his pores, and the heat of his body envelopes me.

Holy fuck.

I never imagined anything could ever top the

feeling of feeding... but this... this is unworldly. My eyes roll into the back of my head as I let him take me... all of me.

And then, it happens.

Instantaneously, it feels like the room is spinning around me, and I forget about my existence. I shout so loud it sends vibrations into his muscles and against my palms on his skin.

I can't speak.

I can't think.

Through some primal instinct, I dig my claws into his neck and pull his face to mine.

I'm about to feed like I've never fed before when our eyes lock, and for the first time, I stop myself.

How... How is this possible? Not once in my entire life have I ever been able to reject a meal. I've stopped halfway, sure, but not before even starting.

Why is this happening? Deep down, do I think he might try to do the same? And if he does, who will win? Maybe this all boils down to survival instincts.

With him still on top of me, I look into his eyes, searching for something.

What does he want from me? Why hasn't he tried to feed?

"It's okay," he says softly. "Take some. You need it more than me."

Is he offering to share some of his life force? What the fuck is going on? Who is this guy? Maybe it's a setup... a trick. He'll turn on me the moment I try.

But the sweet smile on his lips tells me otherwise. Slowly, he presses his plush lips against mine and exhales. The feeling is beyond confusing. Although I can feel the energy exploding inside of me, I'm not the one pulling it in—he's expelling it, and it's enough to drive me mad.

So mad, in fact, that I lose control.

Without warning, I flip him onto his back, grab him by the hair, and suck on his lips as hard as I can. A seductive purple mist spills out of his mouth and into mine.

The taste... the power... It's indescribable.

Unable to control myself, I suck harder, and harder until black lines spiderweb across his face. He stares up at me, a look of terror in his eyes, but I can't stop.

And he's too drained to stop me.

If you don't stop now, you'll kill him.

But I can't...

It feels too fucking good.

His face flushes to a powder white and his eyes glaze over.

Shit.

Unable to stop inhaling, I push myself off as hard as I can and land at the opposite end of the room. The moment I look toward the bed, reality sinks back in and my stomach forms a knot.

His body, pale to the point of being translucent, lies still.

Did I kill him?

In a panic, I rush to the bed.

"Ace?"

His hollow eyes stare at the overcast sky.

"Ace?" I shout.

I place my ear over his lips, feeling his faint breath against my skin.

He's still breathing.

Buck naked, I climb back on top of him and press my lips against his.

Nothing. Why isn't he trying to feed? He needs to take some of his life force back.

I pull away, staring him cold in the eyes. "You need to take some," I say.

A groan escapes his mouth, and he licks his dry, cracked lips.

He's too weak.

"Fuck," I mutter under my breath.

What the hell am I supposed to do? How do you force an incubus to feed if they don't have the energy to? I'm beating myself up for not knowing how to share some of my life force. How did Ace do that?

It doesn't matter. You're running out of time.

I bite my lip, trying to sort through the dozens of thoughts running through my mind. I search the room, the hollow ceiling, the clouds, and then look back down at Ace.

If there's one thing Ace and I share in common, it's succubi survival instinct. He may have been able to control himself with me earlier, but now that he's on the verge of going comatose, nothing will stop this demon from feeding if he's offered a meal... not even me.

It's a risk, but what choice do I have?

Swallowing my panic, I bring out my Lure. It feels forced and unnatural given that my target is hardly moving, but he needs to want this more than anything. Breathing out slowly, I climb on top of him, preparing to feed again. Although I can't know what he's thinking, his rapid heartbeat against my palm tells me he wants this.

I tease him, over and over again, until he's too excited to lay still.

Although he can't vocalize it, I can tell he's experiencing euphoria. I sense it. It's invisible energy generated by my Lure. It leaves my fingertips and enters him through my firm touch, then seeps out of his body and envelops us both.

I feel a similar ecstasy with feebles, but with Ace, the sensation is magnified beyond belief.

Holy shit... What would have happened if we had both used our Lures on each other before sex?

I drop my chest against his and kiss him hard.

This time, he doesn't hold back.

The strength of his inhale is enough to make me think he might suck out my lungs. A loud, high-pitched sound hums between us as a colorful mist licks his chin and slips into his mouth.

His muscular hands grab me by the back of the

head as his cheeks sink in, making it impossible for me to pull away.

Is this it? Is he going to suck me dry?

The black lines across his face disappear as he continues to inhale my life force, and right when I'm about to start yelling in my head for someone to come save me, he pushes me off and sucks in a deep breath as if emerging from the ocean.

His eyes open wide, looking burnt orange under the evening sky.

"Holy shit," he says.

I wipe my lips, not quite understanding how he managed to stop. When it was my turn, I almost killed him.

What the hell is wrong with me?

"Are you okay?" I ask, climbing off and reaching for my clothes.

He doesn't answer, and it almost looks like he's holding back vomit. Was stopping difficult for him?

I fasten my bra and slip my shirt back on. "Why did you do that?"

I don't have to elaborate on my question for him to know what I'm talking about—he knows. Allowing me to feed off him was a huge risk. I don't mean to come across as rude or even ungrateful for what he did, but it was foolish and impulsive. Had I not been able to stop myself, his blood would have been on my hands. And for that, I resent him. I almost killed the guy, and I could have died trying to undo the damage I caused.

"You needed it," he says plainly.

I scoff. "I could have done without it." Wiping my face with both hands, I say, "You could have gotten yourself killed."

A sly smile decorates his face. "I knew what I was getting into when I found you."

"*Found*?" I say. "Found insinuates I was lost in the first place, and you don't know a thing about me."

He averts his gaze.

Goddamn it. Is he a stalker? Does he want something from me, too? Cassidy the witch wasn't shy about expressing why she'd sought me out, so why should Ace's intentions be any different?

What does this asshole want from me?

"Don't do that," he says.

"Don't do what?" I snap.

"Don't create an entire scenario in your head and assume you know what I'm doing here."

For the first time in a long time, I'm at a loss for words. It's like the guy can read my mind.

"You saved my life," he says.

I project rage through my stare. "Only because I almost killed you."

He stays quiet, and instead, climbs off the bed and slips back into his pants. "Your father asked me to keep an eye on you."

I clench my fists. "My father? How would you know anything about my father?"

He sighs. "You were supposed to figure this out

on your own, Alexis."

I'm taken aback by his use of my first name.

"But, you know"—he twirls a finger in the air—"with the end of the world approaching and all, I'd say we're running out of time for you to figure it out."

"What are you talking about?"

His eyes linger on me longer than necessary. "What do you know of your birth parents, Alexis?"

Turning away, I shrug. In my eyes, my biological parents, whoever they were, were cowards. Why else abandon me at the edge of a forest with a doll to protect me? Don't get me wrong—I'm glad they did. Otherwise, I would have never been raised by the man and woman who found me.

To me, they are my true parents, and I couldn't have asked for better ones.

He must sense my resentment and moves toward me, exuding nothing but confidence.

"I knew your real father," he says.

I'm not sure whether to believe him or punch him in the face for making such a bold statement.

"His name was Eros."

He pauses, almost as if for effect. Is this supposed to mean something to me? Elevating my chin, I cross my arms and stare back. Am I getting defensive? Maybe. This guy, who I've known for all of a few hours, is telling me he knew my biological father.

No one's ever spoken about my biological

parents. It's as if they disappeared after handing me over to the village.

I hope they did. Anyone who abandons a child like that—

"You have no idea," Ace says.

No shit.

If I did, I wouldn't be standing here letting him waste my time like this.

"Eros was the son of Ares and Aphrodite. He was the Greek god of love and sex."

My jaw twitches.

I'm too stunned to say anything, so instead, I burst out laughing. "Fuck off. You can't stand there and tell me that my father's a god. That's the most ridiculous thing I've ever heard." My laughter subsides and I glower at him, raising a stiff finger. "And if you think I'm dumb enough to believe—"

"What reason would I have to lie to you?" he cuts me off.

"Oh, I don't know," I say. "To boost my self-esteem? To get even more intense sex out of me?"

I feel like a psycho as the words come out of my mouth. I'm not making much sense, but nothing makes sense to me anymore.

"He and your mother, a succubus demon like you, procreated out of pure sexual desire for one another."

"Procreated," I repeat. "So I'm a procreation."

I'm stalling. This is way too much for me to take in.

"Eros returned to Mount Olympus and couldn't care for you. And your mother, well, everyone knows what happens to children born as demigods. They're hunted and killed for their power."

My head spins, making me feel like I ate shrooms.

His lips move slowly as he speaks, and I wonder if maybe I died seconds ago. Maybe he sucked me dry and none of this is real.

"Your parents didn't want to abandon you, Alexis."

An indescribable rage boils my insides. "How would you even know all of this? Why would a god entrust a demon as filthy as an incubus to carry this secret?"

I hate how calm he is. He acts as if nothing in the world bothers him. Either that, or he truly is that understanding, which makes him a stand-up guy.

"I was there that day... when they carried you to the edge of the forest."

Although I don't want to believe a word he's saying, I can't help but want to hear all about it.

"I was foolish back then... running from a mob of angry husbands whose wives I'd deflowered."

"Deflowered." I scoff. "Are you always so poetic?"

"I'm trying to be respectful," he says. "I can say fuck if you prefer."

My eyes dart toward his groin area. "Yeah, I'd

prefer that."

Fuck. Stay focused, Alexis. Don't let this asshole brainwash you.

"I was near the edge of the forest when I saw them saying goodbye to you. Your mother kissed your forehead, wrapped you up in a beige hemp sheet, and placed a strange-looking doll in your arms. She said something about Alice keeping you safe."

I gape at him. No one else in the world, other than the family who raised me, knows about Alice. Nor about the hemp sheet. Papa gave this blanket to me when I was old enough to understand the significance of it. Instead of interrogating him on how he could have possibly known about any of this, I open my mind and listen, something that doesn't come easily to me.

"I stepped on a branch, inadvertently capturing their attention. Your father turned to me, his eyes filled with tears, and he raised a hand like he was about to make me vanish with a click of his fingers. Your mother stopped him, saving my life, and asked if I could keep an eye on you to ensure that one day, when you were ready and powerful enough to defend yourself from the world, you'd know who your real parents were."

I blink, unable to speak.

"How do you think it is that I can teleport?" he asks.

With tight lips, I shrug.

"Your father gave me the gift in exchange for my loyalty. He said he needed me to be able to follow you anywhere you went."

He pauses, a heavy silence weighing down on us.

Could this be true?

Am I, in fact, a demigod?

The thought sounds preposterous.

"If you were so keen on protecting me," I say, "then why'd you try to steal the *Book of Origin* from me in Adam's house? Loyalty to my father and theft don't exactly mesh well."

"I was trying to protect you from yourself," he says.

Humming, I rub my chin. "Okay, then explain to me why you waited this long to show yourself. I've been able to protect myself for centuries. Why wait until now?"

"Well," he says, intertwining his fingers. "You haven't been ready, Alexis. You've been living a life of anger and selfishness for a long time. Can you imagine the damage you could have caused knowing you were a demigod?"

I swallow hard, pushing away awful memories from my past.

"I came close several times," he continues. "You were getting better at controlling your anger, but then Jamal died, and after that, well..." His forehead wrinkles like it's obvious, which it is.

I part my lips, but nothing comes out.

Jamal.

I'm well aware that I went downhill after his death.

"I worried you might get yourself killed," he finally adds.

Ace seems to know everything about me. How did I not know I was being followed for so long?

With wobbly legs, I move toward the bed and plop myself down, feeling both overwhelmed and depleted.

"Holy shit…" I breathe. "I'm a fucking demigod."

CHAPTER 27

Drax won't stop going on about how now, I can rule the world. I've tried explaining to him that I have no idea what this means or what I'm capable of. He insists that I should be able to teleport like Ace.

"I mean, if your dad gave him that ability, it means it's in your blood, right? Can you maybe teleport me back to San Halos?"

This is the third time in the last ten minutes that Drax asks me to bring him back to San Halos. Why is he so adamant about it? What isn't he telling me? He's never this eager to go anywhere. The guy could easily spend an entire week on a sofa.

"What's going on with you?" I ask. "You're obviously not out of weed—" I make my eyes go big at the bag of green on the bed. Lucky for him, Mr. Mushroom hates the smell of it; otherwise, I'd be yelling at Drax to keep his shit away from my dog. "So, what is it you need from there? You do realize that there are vampires everywhere, right? And that Jamieson might be looking for me? I'm even willing to bet he has a bounty on my head." I laugh at the thought. "Ironically."

The man who used to pay me to kill people must have some other hit man or hit woman trying to track me down. Let them try. I'll tear out their throat with two fingers before they can even say, *Found you.*

Despite my ego, I'm not dumb enough to go back yet. Don't get me wrong—I will. San Halos is my home, but with the world going to shit and all... it's important that we focus on the task at hand and not get distracted by the idea of someone trying to kill me.

Drax sucks hard on his lit joint and sends a thick cloud of smoke toward the sky. "I may or may not have borrowed money from a Krim demon."

I ball my fists until my claws puncture the skin of my palms. "You *what?*"

Everyone knows how dangerous Krim demons are, especially when it comes to money. They're even more greedy than Gortons in that they'll kill anyone who gets between them and their fortunes. What makes them one of the most dangerous demons, however, is that they possess the ability to enter anyone's dream and do what they please with them. Heart attack while sleeping? Chances are it's the result of a Krim demon.

Apparently, succubi and incubi are also known for entering dreams, but I've never mastered that skill. I prefer real-life interaction.

If this guy were anything other than a Krim

demon, I'd likely deal with the situation through violence, but what's terrifying about these demons is that they're not solid form, per se. They reside in hosts—often feebles coming out of comas—and stay there until they want something shinier. So even if you kill what looks to be a Krim demon, all you're doing is killing the shell of a feeble.

All of this to say: no one should ever make a deal with a Krim demon, period. I thought Drax knew better than that.

"How much are we talking about?" I ask.

"Twenty thousand," he says.

A few days ago, I would have lashed out and called him a good-for-nothing lizard. I wouldn't have meant it, of course, but sometimes my anger gets the best of me. Today, however, I'm a multimillionaire, which means a few thousand bucks is pennies to me.

I scoff. "Why didn't you say so? You know I have the money—"

His lips stretch into a guilty smile that makes my stomach sink. "Actually, no one has money right now." He raises his phone. "Internet's gone. Cell has no reception."

Mouth agape, I turn to Ace. "What about you?"

He shakes his head. "Nothing on my end, either. You think Jamieson is behind this?"

I don't know what to think, but I wouldn't put it past him. This is why I wanted to pull my cash out before giving him the chance to manipulate his bank puppets into clearing my money.

I rush to the nearest light switch and flick it on. Nothing.

"Could be our location," I say. "Maybe San Halos is fine."

"I doubt this is Jamieson's doing," Drax says. "What would he have to gain cutting all power? Besides, I know the guy's got reach, but I doubt he has *that* much."

I don't think it's Jamieson either, but it doesn't matter. What matters is the situation we're in now, thanks to Drax's thoughtlessness. Infuriated, I throw my hands up in the air, and Mr. Mushroom runs under the bed. "Why the fuck did you borrow money if you couldn't pay him back?"

"To find you," Drax says, and I feel like an asshole. "You went missing, Alexis. I thought maybe someone had gotten to you. Rachel and I portaled back to San Halos to figure stuff out, and this guy said he was the best of the best and that he'd locate you within twenty-four hours."

"Well, he sucks at his job, because—" And then it hits me. "Where'd you find this guy?"

Drax shrugs. "There was a poster at the entrance of our apartment building. Said if anyone needs to find someone, to give him a call."

I roll my eyes so hard it hurts. "Were you high, Drax? When you called the guy?" I don't give him the time to answer. "How convenient that a poster with some bounty hunter would appear the day after I go missing. Let me guess... He asked you for something of mine."

Drax parts his lips, and I know he's about to say yes, so I stick out a flat palm.

"You got screwed big time, buddy. Not only did you help Jamieson find me, you fucking paid him to do it!"

Everyone looks away, no doubt sensing the fury coming off me. It all makes sense now. Those vampires who interrupted Veerka and me weren't sent by Lucius—they were Jamieson's men and they got tipped off by Drax without him even knowing it.

"Great," I say, pacing back and forth. "Fucking great. I could be found at any time." I whip a hand toward Drax. "And why the fuck are you trying to get back to San Halos if you don't have the money to pay the guy?"

Again with the guilty look. "I wouldn't worry so much, Alexis. I'm sure that with everything going on, Jamieson is too busy to come looking for you. And I intended to ask you for the money, but now that everything's shut down, well, I figured I'd offer him your bike as payment."

My jaw drops. Is he for real? This can't be happening.

"You have lots of money now," Drax says. "You can buy another one."

"And you didn't think of maybe... I don't know, asking me?"

"There's a war going on, Alexis. I didn't want to

add to your stress. I figured I'd get this taken care of and then I'd tell you about it... you know... after."

The rational part of my brain understands where he's coming from, but the emotional side is about ready to tear him a new one.

Inhaling a deep breath, I do my best to talk Red down. Getting angry won't solve the problem. Despite how pissed off I am with Drax, I don't want him to die in his sleep.

"When's the payment deadline?" I ask.

"For who?" he says, heavy lids fluttering above bloodshot eyes.

"The one who's going to fucking kill you, Drax! Can you please take a break from your fucking pot, for like, twenty-four hours? Is that too much to ask?"

It's obvious the thought of it is hurting him, but it's only fair. I set aside my drinking problem to focus on saving the world. He could at least do the same.

Sighing, he crushes his joint over the top of an empty chip bag and throws the rest of it inside.

"Tonight," he says, one last cloud of smoke bursting out of his lungs.

Smiling to avoid blowing another fuse, I shake my head. The timing couldn't be worse. Rachel's gone to who knows where, and when she returns, we won't be here. Then again, she seems adept at locating me no matter where I am, which, for the first time, is a relief.

With hands planted on my hips, I turn to Ace. "How many people can you bring with you when you do your, you know"—I twirl a finger at him—"teleportation thing?"

His eyes scan the room. First, he glances at Mr. Mushroom, then at Riskus, who looks like he's grieving, and then at Drax. No doubt this is the first time he's had to consider something like this, which means it's never been done.

"I'm not sure," he admits. "I've never done it."

"Can't he do one person at a time?" Drax asks.

My focus shifts to Mr. Mushroom, whose snout is sticking out from underneath the bed, and then onto Riskus. Bringing these two along would put them in harm's way, and Rachel would never forgive me if something ever happened to Riskus.

Careful to remain sympathetic, I move toward Riskus. "Hey, man," I say.

His watery eyes roll up at me and his pointed ears wiggle.

"I know Rachel's usually the one who makes portals, but I noticed you have some of that powder on you."

He glances over at Ace, who's staring at him, and then back at me and nods.

"Do you have magic abilities, too?" I ask.

Again, he nods, though he doesn't seem overly confident. I'm assuming his abilities aren't quite as advanced as Rachel's. If I were to guess, I'd say he amplifies her magic but doesn't support it.

"If I asked you and Mr. Mushroom to stay behind, would you be able to make a protection spell?"

Without a word, he nods again, and this time, his long nose wiggles up and down.

Although I don't want to leave Mr. Mushroom behind, I think he'll be much safer in this torn-down motel than anywhere in San Halos.

A few leaves blow into the room from above, bringing along with it the scent of lavender. I move toward the bed, bend down, and call Mr. Mushroom over. He comes running to me like his life depends on it and I scoop him up.

"I won't be long, okay my little Shnookums?" I plant a firm kiss on his forehead and he squints with his ears folded back. I pet him hard and he licks the side of my face. "Riskus here'll take good care of you, okay?"

He licks my face again, almost as if telling me he'll be fine.

With his body still tucked in the elbow of my arm, I yank at the bed's blankets to form a pile. "There you go, you cute little fucking nincompoop."

I can sense everyone's judgmental gazes, but I don't care. Mr. Mushroom and I understand each other. He knows that no matter what I call him, I mean it in the most loving way.

He pants, his snout widening into what resembles a smile, and lets out a high-pitched bark.

"Yes, I promise," I say.

Again with the stares.

"Would you guys stop staring at us? He wants to make sure I stay safe."

Riskus climbs up onto the bed, a feat that requires great effort for such a short creature, and cuddles up next to Mr. Mushroom. It's downright adorable and makes leaving that much more difficult.

"Riskus, make sure—"

But before I can finish telling him to watch over Mr. Mushroom, he throws a fine powder over his head, and a green energy sphere forms around them, encompassing the entire motel bed.

"Holy shit," Drax says, moving away before the magic sears his ass.

From behind the green barrier, Riskus grins, pats Mr. Mushroom on the head, and says in his squeaky voice, "Safe."

I'm too impressed to say anything, so I pucker my lips and nod slowly.

"Well, that's settled," Ace says. "You two ready to go?"

"Can you guarantee one of us won't end up part fly?" I ask.

He smirks. "No, I can't."

Drax opens his mouth to protest, but I cut him off. "In and out, you hear me, Drax? Let's find this guy and make him an offer. Once that's done, we come back, you got it?"

His jaw hangs slack, a look that could easily be

mistaken for condescension. "That was the plan."

"And I expect you to repay me when this is done," I say.

He frowns like a teenager told they can't use their parents' car. I don't mean it—I could give two shits about twenty grand at the moment—but I don't want him thinking he can get away with stunts like these and expect me to get him out of trouble with my riches.

Hey, I like the sound of that.

My riches.

Then again, my riches depend on this war. If the End of the Divide goes full-blown, vampires will jump at the opportunity to take absolute control of the Underworld. If that happens, all the money in the world won't be enough to protect me.

CHAPTER 28

The three of us stand in silence atop PolyKure Inc—a multibillion-dollar industry owned by San Halos's *second* wealthiest man, Ronald McGuire. Jamieson is number one. And the only reason Ronald's name is relevant—it certainly isn't important—is because PolyKure Inc's headquarters happens to be the second tallest building in the city.

The view is beyond words. A sense of calm washes over me as I gaze down at the city. The sun, or at least what remains of it, bounces off thousands of glass windows, making the entire city look like a giant diamond. It gives off a warm, yellow hue that makes me forget how dangerous San Halos can be. It's almost like taking an average picture and applying a colorful filter over it, or laying on a thick layer of high gloss polyurethane over an old worn-out coffee table.

It's magnificent.

While sitting atop skyscraper buildings isn't new to me, it isn't something I've done all that often at sunset. Being that I'm not allowed to show my magic to feebles, I soar through the clouds late at night.

It's funny how I used to fly up onto nearly every building in the city except this one. Why? Jamieson would have blown a fuse if I were caught anywhere near this building. It's not like he'd ever find me on the rooftop. The guy doesn't even know I'm a succubus.

Well, half-succubus, apparently.

Then again, maybe he *does* know. Maybe he's known all along and rather than saying anything, he played stupid. There's a reason the asshole owns half the city. He may be a two-faced prick, but he's a businessman, and he's far from stupid despite my innate desire to perceive him as a half-brained monkey.

Below, people run around like a bunch of lost ducks, though from up here, they look more like ants inside a man-made colony.

Yellow taxis drive chaotically, zooming past parked cars and almost hitting pedestrians. Despite their unnecessary speed and obvious rage, taxi drivers are without a doubt the best drivers out there. They know the dimensions of their car and have no qualms about brushing past someone, or something, with their side mirrors millimeters away from the other guy.

That takes talent.

A cool breeze sweeps through the air, creating waves in my long black hair. I pull it all back, relieved by the weight it takes off my shoulders, and pull it up into a ponytail.

I glance sideways at Drax, and he smirks. I don't have to say anything for him to know what I'm thinking. This is the reason I always keep several elastics on my wrists. When I want my hair out of my face, I want it out *now*. He once told me that keeping elastics on my arm makes me look like a prepubescent teenager wearing old-school goth bracelets. Coincidentally, this also happened around the same time I told him to go fuck himself.

All right, I may have said that *after* he insulted my emergency elastic habit.

"So where does this guy live?" I ask, gazing at the insect infestation below.

Every few seconds, a car honks, but from up here, it's almost inaudible.

"On Fourth Avenue," Drax says, pointing down in its general direction.

"Apartment building?" I ask.

He nods. "If I can get a second to talk to him—"

"Yeah," I say dismissively. "We need to get down to the bank, first."

"Thought you didn't want to be seen," Drax says.

I don't, but the longer I let my money sit in there, the closer I get to losing all of it. There's a good chance Jamieson already got involved after I told him to go fuck himself. He wanted Veerka's sapphire necklace for reasons I have yet to understand, and I didn't deliver it."

"If only Rachel were here right about now," I say. "I'd have her morph me into someone else."

"You think anyone will recognize you?" Ace asks.

"It's possible," I say.

Deep down, I know it's more than possible. After the stunt I pulled on Jamieson, no way is he letting me off the hook. Whether he wants his money back or my head on a silver platter, I'll have to be careful. The thought of taking him out myself has crossed my mind, but the issue with that is that Jamieson has a following like no other. If I kill him, there's no telling how many crazed feebles—or vampires, now that I know he's working with them—will come after me.

"And how exactly do you expect to pull twenty thousand dollars out of the bank without alerting anyone?" Ace asks.

Gazing down at the speeding taxi, I cross my arms. "Quickly."

Admittedly, this idea is a bit rash. Although walking into a bank and demanding to extract money might sound simple enough, it isn't. Not when it comes to large sums like that. What I need is to get in touch with Ouru and find a way to transfer my funds to offshore accounts without anyone noticing. He knows a tech genius who has the means to do this. All I need is the time, which I know is limited.

"Maybe you should try using the machine first,"

Drax says.

I don't bother asking him why he'd suggest such a weird approach. I know how Drax thinks, and the suggestion makes sense. Why waste my time and risk my life walking up to a teller when there's a possibility that Jamieson has already emptied my account? If I go to the bank machine, I'll know right away. I'd much rather check my balance online, but it turns out that isn't a possibility.

What I'd like to know is why my cell service and internet aren't working. If Ace's phone isn't working, it either means the problem isn't personal or it's related to the magical war. Did someone shut down the internet and cellular towers to prevent feeble communication?

I rub my chin, pondering this over.

It would make perfect sense.

If anything, it's brilliant. What better way to divide feebles than to cut off their primary source of communication?

"Ace, care to take me down?" I ask.

I'd fly down, but it's broad daylight and someone would spot me. Besides, if things get out of hand, having Ace by my side is a huge bonus. At the speed of light, he can transport us anywhere.

It's a lot easier to convince feebles that they hallucinated someone disappearing than it is to convince them that the horned demon with wings they saw wasn't real.

"Hey," Drax cuts in. "What about me?"

"Were you not paying attention to anything I told you earlier? Feebles can see demons in their true forms right now."

He grimaces and throws his chin toward the city. "Um, you sure about that?"

With my toes sticking off the ledge, I peek down below. Among countless feebles are demons of all colors, shapes and sizes, and no one is freaking out.

"The Elders must have countered the spell," Ace says.

"Fine, you can come," I say.

Ace steps forward, locks his arms around ours, and everything disappears.

When I open my eyes again, I'm standing in the bank's bathroom with Drax and Ace next to me.

"Well this is going to look awkward," I say.

Ace smirks, no doubt understanding that I'm referring to the three of us walking out of a bathroom together.

"Wait here," he says, and disappears instantly.

When he returns, a soft swooshing sound bounces off the bathroom tiles and he places a black ball cap on my head. "This might help."

"Thanks." I push it down as far as I can and reach for the bathroom's door handle.

Fortunately, the bank's corridor is empty when we step out, but I make it a point to keep my head lowered to avoid the cameras. If Jamieson is still looking for me, he no doubt has someone accessing surveillance cameras throughout all of San Halos.

Did I go too far by crossing Jamieson? Now that I know he's working with the vampires, I question whether I've pushed my luck. All my life, I've done everything in my power to avoid pissing off the vamps, yet here I am... having done it again.

If only I could talk to Veerka.

I need to know what's happening on her end.

What if the vampires aren't even responsible for this? What if it's someone else?

I march down the bank's hall with Ace and Drax following behind and make my way to the bank machine farthest from the tellers' counter. Angry clients protest with clenched fists as the teller tries to explain something to them.

Is the internet outage also affecting accounts? Shit.

I hope not.

Quickening my steps, I hurry to the machine and insert my debit card, lowering my head so my ball cap shadows my face. I sense someone walking behind us, so I glance sideways to check it out.

A man with a gold chain and a big tattoo on his neck eyeballs me but keeps walking. I'm about to face the machine again when I realize I know this guy.

"You," I breathe, and Clock Dragon does that same thing I did—a double take.

I was so caught up in my head that my brain didn't register who he was when I first saw him. His eyes pop out a bit and he takes a step back. The guy fears me, which says a lot considering he works for the vampires.

It looks like he's about to run, so I snatch him by the collar and slam him against the bank machine.

So much for keeping a low profile.

Several eyes turn our way, so I keep my face close to his and both Drax and Ace move in, shielding us from view.

"Where the fuck is it?" I hiss.

He scrunches his nose as if I just ate a can of tuna, which I most certainly did not.

"Lady, I don't know what you're talkin' about." He reaches for my wrist, and although mine is half the size of his, it's a hundred times stronger.

Pathetic feeble.

"You get one warning," I say, my fangs slowly coming out.

Control yourself, Alexis. There are feebles around.

"The fuck do you want from me?" he says, still squirming. "You said you'd leave me alone after I did you a solid. I did what you asked. You're gonna get me killed, you know that?"

Footsteps echo behind us, and Drax clears his throat. "Um, Alexis. Security coming at three o'clock."

"Six o'clock," Ace corrects, and I fight the urge to roll my eyes. "Technically—"

"Would you two shut up?" I hiss.

The footsteps grow louder, and although I

refuse to turn around and look at the guards, I can tell there are three coming my way.

"Where the fuck is the amulet and the book?" I say. "I swear to Athena herself, if you don't answer me, I'll fly you straight up through this goddamn ceiling and crush your skull. I don't give a shit if anyone sees—"

"The book?" he says, looking confused. "As in the *Book of Origin*?"

My grip tightens around his throat, and I bare my teeth at him. "Yeah, that book. I know those slimebag vampires have at least half of it, so you're going to tell me exactly—"

"Lady, you got it all wrong," he says, almost laughing now. "You're tellin' me you ain't the one who got the book?"

I'm too shocked and confused by his reaction to keep squeezing his throat, so I let go.

My confusion must be written all over my face. He gives me his cocky smirk like I don't know shit and sucks on his front teeth. "Man, I had a feeling it wasn't you."

"What are you talking about?" I ask.

"Hey!" comes an authoritative male voice. "What's going on over here?"

Although I still refuse to turn away from Clock Dragon, or Adrian if I recall correctly, I can picture the guards perfectly—puffed chests, hands on their useless batons, and frowns so pronounced their brows protrude from their faces.

Clock Dragon glances toward them and shakes his head. Then, in a whisper, he says, "The vampires are blaming the fae for this, and apparently, you guys are blamin' them. If I didn't know any better, I'd say someone set you up." With pouted lips, he throws his chin out at me as if to emphasize my stupidity. "And if you guys don't smarten the fuck up soon, you're gonna get us humans killed."

A hint of anger flashes across his face.

I blink once, then twice.

I've been around enough feebles to know when they're lying, and Clock Dragon isn't lying.

"Step away from the man and put your hands in the air," comes that same voice.

Dumb wannabe cop.

If I turn around—and if Jamieson is after me—they might call for backup or things might get heated. So instead, I stick my hands up and take a step back from Clock Dragon.

"All good here, boys. Just friends sorting out their differences. You know how it is."

"Turn around and put your hands in the air," that same voice repeats.

He sounds more menacing this time, like he's about to whip out his gun even though it's against protocol unless there's an immediate threat, and it's not like I have a knife against Clock Dragon's throat. Or maybe they do know who I am, and they've been instructed to take me in dead or alive.

Drax leans into me. "Might wanna act fast. Guy

on the left is reaching for his gun."

"Guy on the *right*," Ace says and Drax shoots him a death glare.

Well, it looks like busting upward and through the ceiling of this bank might be my one option. It'll be much easier telling the Council of Elders that my actions directly resulted from wanting to deliver pertinent information relevant to this war than to tell them I needed to crush a few skulls in front of witnesses.

Sighing, I roll my head until my neck cracks, and Clock Dragon grimaces at the sound. "See you later," I say, prepared to grab Drax and Ace around their torsos and shoot us all upward.

Although the plan sounds dangerous—I mean, it's pretty reckless to smash through layers upon layers of concrete and brick—I have it all figured out. I'm agile, so midair, I'll wrap my legs around Drax and Ace and use my fists to break apart an opening for us.

The last thing I want is for Drax's head to get in the way. He may be fae, but his skull isn't made of iron and he isn't immortal. He wouldn't come out of it alive.

Or, I could stop trying to be so badass and ask Ace to get us the fuck out of here.

Boring.

But it's the smarter plan.

The second I lean into him, I hear a gun being cocked. "Get on the floor, now!"

I bite down hard, doing everything in my power to keep my wings and horns from coming out.

If this son of a bitch wants to threaten me at gunpoint, so help me God—

But then, something unexpected happens.

Everything goes quiet... so quiet that I think I've gone deaf. In front of me, Clock Dragon stares straight forward like he's about to seize, or like he's made eye contact with Medusa.

He looks... frozen.

I frown at him, waiting for his expression to change, but it doesn't.

"Um, Alexis," Ace says.

Slowly, I turn around to find people frozen in place throughout the bank.

"What the fuck..." Drax breathes.

I turn back to face Clock Dragon, my index finger hovering inches away from his face. Maybe if I poke him, he'll move. But before I can do that, his skin turns blue and breaks apart into what appear to be illuminated shards of glass.

An overpowering swooshing sound spreads throughout the bank. Around us, people break apart into bright bits.

"What the hell is going on?" I say.

The speckles of light swirl upward, and as they slip through the overhead ceiling, bodies disappear entirely, leaving a few people to wander about as confused as I am.

And by people, I mean shadow dwellers.

"No fucking way," I say.

Ace steps forward, his gaze scanning the almost empty bank. "I can't believe it. They pulled off the Interruptus spell."

Drax looks both terrified and excited. "What does that mean? No more humans? Freedom for us? Or, wait a minute. My dealer's human. Shit." He paces, his heavy footsteps resonating off the bank's marble walls. "And what about the internet? I mean, I know a few Gorton demons that work in the industry, but everyone knows that feebles manage all of that. This isn't good. This is definitely not good." His pacing quickens, and the moment he's arm's length away from me, I slap him across the face.

His face goes blank.

"Would you snap out of it and calm?" I say. "Freaking out won't fix any of this."

"Then tell me, genius, what are we supposed to do?"

Ace cuts in. "From what I'm told, an Interruptus spell can't last more than twenty-four hours. And for the council to cast a spell of that magnitude means they're preparing for war."

Drax's big reptilian eyes dart from me to Ace.

"We need to find Rachel," I say. "Hopefully she'll have found Zerachu by now."

A young woman with green skin and pink wings races across the bank, her lanky legs scissoring as her backpack bounces up and down, dropping spell books, a wand, and a pouch of dust.

Ignoring her, I add, "The council is prepared to go to war with the vampires, but if the vampires didn't do this, it means we're fighting the wrong bad guy. Whoever did this wants both sides to suffer. If we don't do something about it, shadow dwellers will start killing each other for nothing, and millions of people will die."

Ace, looking as calm as always, crosses his arms, his leather jacket squeaking. "What do you suggest?"

Although my heart and mind are at war with each other over my racing thoughts, I know what I need to do even though it's the last thing I *want* to do. "First, we deliver my bike to the Krim demon and save Drax's ass. Then, we need to get the vampires and the fae to join forces."

There's a long pause, almost as if we're waiting for some intense theme music to kick in... the kind of music you'd hear at the end of a television series' season finale.

But nothing happens.

Instead, Drax gives me a look that makes me question my sanity.

"What?" I say.

"You make it sound like getting enemies to team up is as easy as cracking a nut."

Ace's eyebrow pulls up. "Cracking a nut isn't—"

Drax waves a scaly hand to shut him up.

I get where Drax is going with this. It won't be

easy. I'm not an idiot. Vampires and fae have been at war for ages. But if Clock Dragon was telling the truth, then whoever caused all of this is *trying* to worsen the conflict, which means shadow dwellers are going to kill each other for nothing.

I have no clue how I'm going to go about uniting the different clans—all I know is that we need to try. It'll get messy, but if we don't do this, things will get even messier.

I stare at my friends, telepathically asking them if they're ready to fight for this cause.

They seem to understand—Drax crosses his thick green arms and nods. Ace stiffens his stance.

We can do this.

I'm shocked by my thoughts. *We* has never been part of my vocabulary. I've always been a lone wolf type of girl. But I know it's time I put that behind me. If we hope to save the world—*wow, I'm on a roll with this heroic stuff*—we need to work together.

The mission itself might sound suicidal, but I like to think we have good odds thanks to our kick-ass team. I have two trustworthy friends willing to fight by my side, a witch with the potential to be as powerful as Zerachu, and, well... me—a demigod.

There's no stopping us.

For the first time in years, I have no desire to chug back a few beers to calm my nerves. Am I worried? A bit. But something inside me says that if we work together, we can do this.

I elevate my chin, offer my boys a sly smile, and

plant my hands on my hips like Supergirl.

"Come on," I say, jerking my head sideways. "Let's stir some shit up."